"All right, Mr. Stoner. I'll hire you on a trial basis. One month."

"I'll be here as long as you need me."

The words were innocuous enough, but somehow he invested them with deeper meaning.

"What does that mean?" Gwen asked.

"I'm a man who has to drift. I'm just passing through."

"I'm not interested in hiring a transient," she said sharply.

The man met her eyes, his gaze clear and steady. "I'll stay as long as you need me. I always do."

Gwen wanted to believe Jake Stoner. She had no choice but to believe him. "All right," she said slowly. "When can you start?" Please, she thought, let it be now.

He held out his hand. "Soon as we shake on it, ma'am."

She didn't want to shake hands with him. She didn't want to touch him. The realization disconcerted her. Jake Stoner was more than the hunk her lawyer Prudence had labeled him. He was overwhelmingly male. If she knew one thing, it was that Jake Stoner spelled trouble. And he worked for her.

Dear Reader,

Remember the magic of the film *It's a Wonderful Life*? The warmth and tender emotion of *Truly, Madly, Deeply*? The feel-good humor of *Heaven Can Wait*?

Well, we can't promise you Alan Rickman or Warren Beatty, but we know you'll be delighted with the latest miniseries in Harlequin Romance®: **GUARDIAN ANGELS**. It brings together all of your favorite ingredients for a perfect novel: great heroes, feisty heroines, breathtaking romance, all with a celestial spin. Written by four of our star authors, this witty and wonderful series features four real-life angels— all of whom are perfect advertisements for heaven!

Already available are *The Boss, the Baby and the Bride* by Day Leclaire and *Heavenly Husband* by Carolyn Greene. This month it's Jeanne Allan's turn with *A Groom for Gwen*— a story of such emotional intensity you'll cry tears of laughter and sadness at its tender humor and heart-wrenching poignancy. Not to be missed in December is Margaret Way's *Gabriel's Mission*.

Have a heavenly read!

The Editors

GUARDIAN ANGELS

Falling in love sometimes needs a little help from above!

GUARDIAN ANGELS

A Groom for Gwen
Jeanne Allan

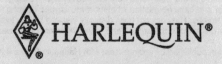

HARLEQUIN®

TORONTO • NEW YORK • LONDON
AMSTERDAM • PARIS • SYDNEY • HAMBURG
STOCKHOLM • ATHENS • TOKYO • MILAN • MADRID
PRAGUE • WARSAW • BUDAPEST • AUCKLAND

For my father,
who knew how to tell a story

ISBN 0-373-03524-1

A GROOM FOR GWEN

First North American Publication 1998.

Copyright © 1998 by Barbara Blackman.

CHAPTER ONE

SLOUCHED against the building, Jake watched the woman come down the street. With her yellow hair, she was pretty as a bald-faced heifer. Somehow Jake knew when he cut the right trail, although Michaels never told him.

Michaels. No first name, just Michaels. The man looked like a greenhorn in his boiled shirt and derby. Jake thought of him as a kind of trail boss for the Almighty, but Michaels was unlike any bible-puncher Jake had known. Those preachers could plumb tucker a man out with their palaver about brimstone and damnation. Michaels, on the other hand, didn't say much, but his piercing blue eyes told Jake that Michaels had experienced more than most men would know in a dozen lifetimes. Those same eyes saw right though a man's hide and counted all his sins.

Jake had plenty of sins to count, he thought, idly admiring the long, graceful legs striding toward him. No sashaying for this woman. Women rigged out in pants no longer startled him, and he studied her from head to toe with masculine appreciation. She was on the slender side, but she had enough womanly curves to please. Jake had never been partial to the big-bosomed women his brother Luther had liked hanging on him. He wished he could see the eyes hidden behind them dark cheaters— sunglasses, they called them now—that everyone wore. From the look on her face, the woman was making a powerful sight of thinking about something more than the tyke in her arms.

Michaels said this was the tenth time. The tenth and

last. Then Jake could present himself at the Pearly Gates. Jake was tired of evil and war and killing and stupidity and greed. Over a century had passed since Jake's time, and mankind had learned nothing. Sometimes Jake thought he didn't even care if he went upstairs or down below. He just wanted out of it. No more anger, sorrow, frustration, worry or caring. He wanted, once and for all time, to simply cease to be.

He'd tried to tell Michaels how he felt, but the other man had already gone. Jake hated that. Michaels came and went like a ghost. Maybe Jake did the same. If this was ten, that meant he'd done nine jobs already, but those jobs, those people, had faded from his memory.

His memories came from his real life.

If people like him had memories.

Funny, what he knew and what he didn't know. Jake knew he'd been gunned down in 1886 while relieving a bank of the responsibility of storing so many banknotes. He didn't know why he hadn't been tossed in the hellfire down below. Michaels never answered questions. He simply sent Jake back to earth to help people.

People like the woman drawing near. Jake straightened and tipped his hat.

The August wind blowing off the high Colorado plains made a mockery of her once neatly combed hair. Gwen blinked the grit from her eyes as a crumpled piece of paper blew across the Trinidad street and bounced off her grimy canvas shoe. Dust coated her face. So much for bucolic fantasies. Someone should have warned her country living meant wind and dirt and grasshoppers. And smells. Not once had she seen a painting of cows which included cow patties. It was dishonest, is what it was. Not that she was so stupid she couldn't figure out what went in had to come out.

Head bowed against the wind, she muttered, "Insanity, thy name is Gwen Ashton."

Crissie giggled, and tightened her grip around Gwen's neck.

Gwen gave her niece a look of mock reproach. "A big girl who's going to be four years old on her next birthday ought to be walking instead of being carried like a baby."

"I tired," Crissie said matter-of-factly.

"What a shame. I thought we could have some ice cream, but if you're too tired to walk, you must be too tired to eat."

The little girl wiggled. "I want down." On the ground, she beamed a beatific smile at her aunt. "Strawberry ice cream?"

Gwen shuddered ostentatiously. "Strawberry. Yuk." The way the dust swirled around them, they'd be better off ordering chocolate so the dirt, which was bound to stick to the ice cream, didn't show. Not that a little dirt would be such a great disaster. Compared to the rest of the day, a little dirt on ice cream could almost be considered a blessing. And she could certainly use a blessing or two.

"Howdy, Ma'am."

At first the slow, deep drawl didn't register. She didn't know anyone in Trinidad, Colorado, except Prudence. Gwen reminded herself she wasn't living in Denver anymore. Here, everyone probably greeted strangers. Not to reply would be rude. Fixing a polite smile on her face, she turned to the man standing in the shadow of the storefront. He was tall, forcing her to look up past a broad chest and wide shoulders. The smile froze on her face.

The man belonged in a picture book about outlaws and desperadoes. He hadn't shaved in recent history, and dark stubby whiskers accentuated a squared-off jaw which appeared to have been hewn from granite. A devil-may-care smile curved his mouth, but the gray eyes beneath heavy dark brows stayed cool. Gwen managed to say hello.

He removed a battered wide-brimmed black felt hat, revealing shaggy, coal-black hair. "Jakob Stoner, Ma'am. Call me Jake. I guess you need a cowhand."

Gwen clutched her purse with one hand, and Crissie's hand with the other. "Where did you hear that?" Silly question. City folk, jammed one on top of the other in town houses and apartments had privacy. In rural communities news didn't need wires or microwaves to travel faster than the speed of light or whatever traveled fastest.

He shrugged. "Word gets around."

It wasn't much of an answer. "Did Prudence tell you I'm looking for a new ranch hand?"

"Prudence?" Amusement gleamed briefly in his eyes. "Ma'am, I don't think working for you and your husband has anything to do with prudence."

"I don't have a husband." Gwen immediately cursed herself for saying so. Why didn't she just tell him she and Crissie lived in the middle of nowhere, her nearest neighbor resided miles away, and her ranch manager was ill and her only other ranch hand had walked out during the night? The lock on the ranch house door didn't work, the only weapon in the house was an antique buffalo gun which she wouldn't know how to shoot even if it was loaded, and her idea of self-defense was to call a cop if she saw a suspicious-looking stranger. She had no clue how to handle the tall, dark, dangerous-looking man who stood on the sidewalk in front of her.

"You're hurting my hand," Crissie complained.

Gwen released Crissie's hand, but before she could sweep her niece up into her arms, the man squatted down to Crissie's level. "Howdy, pardner."

"I'm Crissie," the little girl announced. "Not pardner."

"My name is Jake." Setting a much-traveled duffel bag on the ground by a beat-up saddle, he solemnly held out his hand. "Howdy, Crissie."

Gwen wanted to snatch Crissie's hand away. Common sense stopped her. Desperate criminals didn't carry luggage and saddles. They didn't abduct nobodies in broad daylight in the middle of town. All she and Crissie had to do was walk away.

At the sight of Crissie's small white hand swallowed up by the large, tanned hand of the stranger, a painful surge of memories swamped Gwen. In her mind's eye she saw Dan marveling at the tiny perfection of his newborn daughter's hands and feet. Monica painting tiny fingernails outrageous shades of fuchsia and lavender. "Crissie." The child's name caught on the painful lump in Gwen's throat. "We have to go."

"Is he gonna get ice cream wid us?" Crissie asked.

"I plan to have the biggest vanilla cone you ever did see."

"I want vanilla." Crissie immediately abandoned her prior preference for strawberry.

"Let's head for the ice cream parlor, pardner." He released Crissie's hand, replaced his hat, and reached for his saddle and bag.

"Just a moment, Mr. Stoner."

He must have heard something in Gwen's voice because he left his things on the sidewalk and stood tall, facing her. "My pa was Mr. Stoner. Since I'll be working for you, Ma'am, you call me Jake."

Gwen ignored the slow, confident smile. "You won't be working for me, Mr. Stoner. I don't hire a perfect stranger."

He shook his head, saying ruefully, "Ma'am, the last thing I've ever been is perfect."

As if that were any recommendation. "Mr. Stoner," Gwen said evenly, "Prudence Owen, the attorney handling the probate of Bert's estate, is finding me an employee."

"I don't think so, Ma'am. If she was, you wouldn't need me."

"I don't need you," she snapped.

"You need me. That's why I'm here. You need a cowboy." He picked up his gear. "I'm a cowboy."

Did he think she was a complete idiot just because she'd never lived on a ranch before? A ranch was nothing more than a business operated outdoors, she repeated to herself for about the millionth time since she'd moved down here. A business about which she knew less than nothing, as became more evident with each passing day. Maybe around here ranchers hired help on such a casual basis. She shook her head, saying under her breath, "Oh boy, Toto, I'm not in Kansas anymore."

He heard the last words. "You come from Kansas?"

"Denver," she said curtly. And almost wished she were back there. But that thought led to too many wishes which could never be granted.

"City of the Plains."

"What?" Her sinuses must be so plugged with dust, they were affecting her hearing. Or pressing on her brain.

"Denver. We used to call her the 'City of the Plains.'"

Gwen took a deep breath and tried to take control of the conversation. She'd hired strangers before. "Why did your former employer let you go?"

"You mean the people I helped before? I left because they didn't need me anymore."

Translation: fired. Downsizing, country style. She had a feeling he didn't have letters of reference. But ranch hands did appear to have their own network. One cowboy in need of a job. One brand-new ranch owner desperately in need of a cowboy. Prudence had howled with mirth when Gwen suggested contacting an employment agency for a ranch hand. When the pretty lawyer finally quit laughing, she said she'd spread the word that the Winthrop ranch needed hands. This cowboy may not have talked with Prudence, but he'd evidently gotten the word.

Gwen scrutinized the man standing easily in front of her. Nothing about his clothing countermanded her impression that a very dangerous man stood before her. No satin shirts or embroidery or sequins for this man. She could only surmise his faded shirt had once been black and the rose-colored scarf tied around his neck had been red. A scarred brown leather belt cinched worn blue jeans around a narrow waist. Leather chaps made his legs look a million miles long. His boots were worn down at the heels and she'd bet they'd never seen a lick of polish.

The squint lines fanning out from the corners of his eyes attested to a life spent working outdoors. Real cowboys didn't have to be bow-legged and spit chewing tobacco. He could be a down-on-his-luck cowboy whose empty pockets had dictated he sleep out of doors the past few nights. He might look less lethal if he shaved.

He patiently endured her inspection, but she was under no illusion that he awaited her conclusions with any anxiety or doubt. He clearly intended to work for her no matter what she thought. This man had a high opinion of his worth. And he knew who had the greater need. His quiet assurance irritated her. "I'm sorry you lost your last job, Mr. Stoner, but I'm afraid you'll have to look elsewhere for a new one. I need some kind of reference or assurance a person knows one end of a cow from the other end before I would considering hiring him. Goodbye, Mr. Stoner, and good luck." It startled

Gwen that a man so relaxed could get his muscles moving so quickly. One second he was beside the building, the next he stood in front of her barring her way.

He held out his hands, palms up, and pointed to a weal running across one palm. "Rope burn. I was twelve and roped an old mossy back steer who had other ideas. I was just stubborn enough to insist he go along with my plans."

She couldn't stop herself from asking, "Did he?"

"Eventually." He stretched out a crooked middle finger. "Broke that when I tried to ride a horse who preferred I walk. This—" he pointed to a scar on the back of his other hand "—is where a Texas cow took exception to me getting between her and her youngun."

The strong, rugged hands fascinated Gwen. No way could she see those hands operating a computer or elegantly holding the stem of a wineglass. Not that the long fingers, the unbroken ones, that is, didn't have an elegance about them. She could see those fingers soothing a timid colt or a nervous mare. She could see them stroking naked skin. An image Gwen quickly shook off. "If you think your catalog of injuries serves as an adequate résumé, you're sadly mistaken. You're clearly unqualified to work on a ranch."

"I'll have to respectfully disagree with you there, Ma'am. I've had lots of experience. And experience is the best teacher."

He had an answer for everything. If she wasn't careful, she'd find herself hiring this modern version of outlaw Jesse James. The truth was, she needed someone who knew cows and horses better than she did. A classification which covered most of the world's population. The solution came to her in a flash. Prudence. "As I told you, Mr. Stoner, Ms. Owen is doing my hiring. We'll go over to her office right now, and see if you can satisfy her as to your qualifications. Not that I'm making any promises about hiring you,'' she added hastily.

He gave her an amused look. ''You'll hire me.''

Prudence took in her stride Gwen's reappearance, this time with a cowboy in tow. ''Have you any identification?'' she asked briskly after Gwen explained their visit.

The man hesitated, then patted his back pocket before slowly pulling out his billfold. He handed it to the lawyer without a word.

Prudence extracted the plastic-coated license and quickly scanned it. ''This seems to be in order.'' She handed the billfold and license to Gwen.

Gwen silently read the information on his driver's license. Jakob Carl Stoner. Six feet, three inches tall. Black hair. Gray eyes. She quickly computed his age. Thirty-one. That surprised her. For some reason, something about his eyes, she'd thought him older. Slotting the license back in his billfold, she glanced up to catch a puzzled look on his face as he stared down at his billfold. A look quickly erased as he noticed her looking at him. Had he expected her to count his money or snoop through his credit cards?

Prudence asked Jake Stoner a number of probing questions. His answers seemed to satisfy the lawyer. Thanking him, she asked the man to wait out in the reception area.

''Well, Gwen,'' she said as soon as the office door closed, ''I'd say you found yourself a cowboy. How did you happen to stumble across him?''

''Stumble is the right word. He was waiting for me down the street. You must have started calling people right after I left here earlier.''

Prudence frowned. ''Actually, I've been so busy, I haven't had a chance to make any phone calls.'' Her brow smoothed out and she shook her head. ''I've lived here most of my life, and I still can't believe how quickly everyone knows everything that's going on."

"You really think it's okay to hire him? You don't think he looks kind of dangerous?"

The lawyer laughed. "I think he's such a hunk I wish I needed a cowhand." She sobered. "He seems to know ranching, and you're darned lucky to find anyone on such short notice. Try him for a few weeks, and see how things work out. If you want, I'll keep looking for another hand for you."

Gwen could hardly say the man made her nervous, so she agreed to try him and stood up to leave.

Prudence leaned back in her chair and pointed a fountain pen at Gwen. "I think what it is, you're used to city boys. This, my dear, is a man."

Gwen didn't need a lawyer to tell her that.

Closing Prudence's door a little more sharply than she intended, Gwen carefully slid on her sunglasses. "All right, Mr. Stoner. I'll hire you on a trial basis. One month. If your work is satisfactory, we'll discuss a long-term arrangement."

"I'll be here as long as you need me."

The words were innocuous enough, but somehow he invested them with deeper meaning. As if he meant more than the fact she needed an employee. As if he knew something she didn't know. She narrowed her eyes behind her dark lenses. "What does that mean?"

"I'm a man who has to drift. I'm just passing through. When you don't need me anymore, I'll leave."

"I'm not interested in hiring a transient," she said sharply. "I've already had one employee run out on me. He didn't even have the courtesy—or nerve—to face me. Slipped a note under my front door last night. I found it this morning. He went to Wyoming. How do I know you won't do the same?"

The man met her eyes, his gaze clear and steady. "I'll stay as long as you need me. I always do."

Rod Heath's eyes had been shifty, looking everywhere but at her. Gwen wanted to believe Jake Stoner. She had no choice but to believe him. "All right," she said slowly. "When can you start?" Please, she thought, let it be now.

He held out his hand. "Soon as we shake on it, Ma'am."

She didn't want to shake hands with him. She didn't want to touch him. The realization disconcerted her. She'd shaken hands with thousands of men in the course of business. Shaking hands with Jake Stoner was no different. Slowly she accepted his extended hand. An electric current zipped up her arm as his work-roughened palm closed around hers. Jake Stoner was more than the hunk Prudence had labeled him. He was overwhelmingly male. Gwen retrieved her hand. If she knew one thing, it was that Jake Stoner spelled trouble. And he worked for her.

He gave her an odd look, but said only, "I'll get my gear." Then he laughed softly and nodded across the room.

Gwen followed his gaze, and her breath caught in her throat. She'd left Crissie with Prudence's receptionist while she consulted the lawyer. Now the child lay sprawled on the floor, sound asleep, one arm curved around an enormous yellow dog.

The dog opened his eyes. One blue eye and one brown eye stared at Gwen. She stood very still, not daring to breathe. Crissie sucked contentedly on her thumb, her head resting on the cowboy's saddle. Gwen prayed her niece wouldn't accidentally annoy the dog in her sleep. Quietly she asked, "Whose dog is that?"

"Mine." A burly man turned from his conversation with the receptionist. "Mack won't hurt her. He loves kids. My wife took off for California with my boys. She isn't coming back and refused to take the dog. I can't take care of Mack, so I have to take him to the pound. Too bad, really. He's a good dog, but almost five years old. People want puppies.''

Gwen gave the huge dog a second look. "What is he?"

The man shrugged. "Near as I can figure, part husky, part golden retriever, and maybe some mastiff or Great Dane. He'd make a good watchdog for your little girl. He's housebroken," the man added quickly.

Gwen walked toward Crissie. The dog raised his head, giving her a fixed look. "You're sure he's friendly?"

"Oh, sure, he won't hurt you."

"Move, Mack. I need to wake up Crissie. Be a good dog, Mack."

The dog slid out from under Crissie's arm and rose to his feet. He gently nudged the sleeping girl. She opened her eyes and giggled. "Mack tickles." She stood up. "Look, Gwen, he likes me. The man said he can come home with me."

"He's been fixed. I got his shot records, his bowls and most of a bag of dog food out in the pickup," the man said hopefully. "I sure hate to think of ol' Mack getting put down. People want puppies."

"So you said." Gwen had no intention of taking the dog.

"Mack's my new bes' friend." Crissie hung on to the dog for dear life.

Gwen eyed the dog dubiously. He seemed to like Crissie, and he might be protection for the young girl. Gwen glanced at Jake Stoner. And for her.

His mouth twitched. "I'll get Mack's gear out of the truck." As he passed Gwen, he said in a voice pitched for her ears alone, "With a dog of that size, you won't have to worry about me attacking you in your bed."

So he wasn't just a cowboy. He was a mind reader, too.

Mack sat in the back seat with Crissie as they headed east out of Trinidad. After eating his ice-cream cone in two gulps, the dog had covetously eyed Crissie's cone, but to Gwen's relief he hadn't snatched it from the little girl. Gwen decided to overlook Mack's licking the ice cream residue off Crissie's face. Crissie hadn't minded. The child had wholeheartedly adopted the dog. Maybe keeping him wouldn't be a total disaster.

"Kids on a ranch can get lonely." Jake Stoner read her thoughts again. "The dog'll make a good playmate and watchdog. You didn't make a mistake taking him, Ma'am."

"If the dog doesn't work out, I'll take him to the dog pound myself." Out of the corner of her eye she saw the amused skepticism on his face. "I will. And don't call me ma'am."

He laughed. "You're stuck with the dog and you know it. I don't recall you ever got around to telling me your name."

"Gwen Ashton."

"Ashton. Your family been ranching around here long?"

"No. I inherited the ranch from a client of mine."

"Ah."

Gwen heard a wealth of meaning in the simple response. "There's no 'ah' about it. I don't care what you've heard, Bert and I were friends. Nothing more."

"I haven't heard anything. Why don't you tell me?"

She didn't need to explain anything to an employee. "I'm a Certified Public Accountant. I worked for a firm up in Denver, and became acquainted with Bert when I started doing his taxes."

Glancing at the puffy white clouds piling one on top of the other over the dark mesa to the south, Gwen thought again how the stark beauty of this countryside went a long way toward explaining how Bert Winthrop, so conscientious about caring for his livestock, could set new standards in lackadaisical when it came to the paperwork involved with running his ranch. All the tax preparers who'd washed their hands of him probably never left their sterile cubicles to breathe deeply of the country air.

"He left you his place because you showed him how to get out of paying the government what he owed?"

"He left me the ranch because I love it as much as he did." Beside the road sunflowers turned their faces to the sun. "I love the beauty and I love the history. I loved hearing Bert talk about his family pioneering out here on the high Colorado plains. They homesteaded and survived grasshopper plagues, Indian scares, bank failures and the 'Dust Bowl' years when the drought was so severe most of the topsoil blew away. Generations of Bert's family were born, lived, and died on the ranch." Gwen smiled reminiscently. "Until I met Bert, I never thought before about history as being someone's uncle or aunt or grandfather. Some of his family actually came out here by way of the Santa Fe trail. Some fought in a Civil War battle down in New Mexico. Did you know there'd been a Civil War fight out here? I didn't."

"The battle of Glorieta Pass."

"That's right. And one of his ancestors hauled freight from a fort in New Mexico to a place up north of here on the railroad."

"Ft. Union to Granada."

"You must be interested in history, Mr. Stoner."

"I've picked stuff up."

"I never realized how fascinating it could be. Some of Bert's relatives kept journals, and I've been reading them. Bert had roots and family which goes back over one hundred years in this area." She slowed the car to make a turn. "I love the journals and wouldn't part with them for a million dollars. I offered to make copies for Gordon, but he's not the least bit interested. Not in them."

"Who's Gordon? Your ex-husband?"

"I've never been married. Gordon Pease is Bert's nephew. He's convinced I manipulated Bert into leaving me the ranch. That I took advantage of a senile old man. If he'd spent ten minutes with Bert in the past year he'd know the last thing Bert was, was senile."

"What was he?"

"Lonely, I suppose."

"So you were kind to him."

"Bert wasn't a pathetic old man who needed befriending," Gwen said indignantly. "He enriched my life."

"He left you a ranch because you listened to him?" Jake Stoner asked, skepticism filling his voice.

"He left it to me because he knew I'd love it. Bert married late, and his wife Sara died early. Bert should have remarried, but he didn't, and all that's left of his family is Gordon. Gordon moved to Colorado about five years ago and moved in with Bert for a short time. According to Bert, Gordon hated the ranch and everything about it. Gordon only wants the ranch because he thinks he can sell it and make a bundle."

"You plan to sell it?"

"Never. All my life I've dreamed of my own home. A big house with a white picket fence. My dad was in the Air Force, and my mom would no more than get unpacked and it was time to pack up again. Mom and my brother Dan loved it, but not me. I wanted to settle. Mom says I take after my Grandmother Ashton. Both my grandfathers had itchy feet. They were always quitting their jobs and moving on to where the grass was sure to be greener. Grandmother Ashton hated it. She used to show me pictures and tell me about the home she grew up in back in Missouri.''

"With a white picket fence?"

"The fence is symbolic," she said impatiently. "Putting down roots, that's what counts. A place where a person belongs. So that no matter where you go, you know home is waiting for you to come back. I want a home which records our lives. I want marks on the wall showing how tall Crissie is at five and ten and fifteen years of age. I want to know that whatever weather I'm dressing for now, I'll be dressing for the same weather five and ten Augusts from now. I want Crissie to be able to plant a tree and watch it grow for years and years." Gwen gave an embarrassed laugh. "Sorry. My brother used to say I was a little irrational on the subject. It probably sounds stupid to a man like you who doesn't like to stay long in one place."

"There was a time when I considered settling down myself. Not too far from here. Even built myself a nice little place and…"

Gwen pulled into the ranch yard and parked the car. Then she turned to see why Jake Stoner hadn't finished his sentence. He was staring in astonishment at Bert's house. Her house. "I know it looks a little strange," she said defensively, "but I like it. The earliest part dates from the early 1880's, and every generation of Bert's family added on to it. This is a house with character."

Jake Stoner stepped out of the car and pivoted slowly on the heel of his boot, scanning the landscape. Squinting into the sun he methodically studied the various ranch buildings one by one. His gaze lit on the small stone house where Lawrence Hingle and Rod Heath, the ranch employees, had lived, then moved on to the earliest section of the main house. "I'll be double-dog damned," he said in quiet disbelief. He looked around again, eyed the mesa in the distance, and roared with laughter.

CHAPTER TWO

AFTER nine trips, Jake ought to be accustomed to being sent back equipped with the basic necessities such as a billfold with the proper driver's license. He should have guessed Michaels would have taken care of the details.

Jake never would have guessed Michaels had a sense of humor. Sending Jake back to his own place. Jake wondered what Gwen would have said if he'd told her he'd built the stone section of the main house and the little stone house he now slept in. He'd chiseled the stone almost square like his pa taught him. The timbers for the porches across the front of both places were freighted in from the mountains. Long hours of back-breaking work. Work he hadn't minded because he'd thought nothing more important than having his own ranch. Being his own man.

Folding his arms behind his head, Jake stared sightlessly at the ceiling. He'd been sixteen when Charlie Goodnight hired him on after the Civil War. Old enough and strong enough to do a man's work. You had to be a man to trail cows up the Goodnight Trail from Texas. He'd never told Charlie he'd run away from home so he wouldn't kill Frank the next time he laid into Jake with the bullwhip. Ma had turned a blind eye to his step-pa's doings. Jake guessed she was scared of living alone. He tried not to think about her much.

He lay on an old iron bed, a sheet and an old faded quilt pulled up to his waist. The bed pushed up against the rock exterior wall. He'd left open the shutters, and shadows from a nearby scraggly pine flickered across the whitewashed lumber which paneled the other three walls. Someone else had put up the interior walls in what he'd built as the bunkhouse.

The main house he'd been building like the one Pa built near the banks of the Guadalupe River. If Jake shut his eyes he could see the Guadalupe making its way past gnarled and knotted bald cypress trees, their limbs covered with moss. Green, soft moss. Like the pillow on his mother's best parlor chair.

Or his boss lady's eyes.

Jake laughed softly. He'd seen the horrified look on her face when Mack's previous owner talked of Mack being put down and knew instantly the dog had found a new home. Gwen Ashton tried to talk tough, but she was soft.

A soft heart wasn't necessarily good. Not if it kept a person from making the tough decisions. Women could feel sorry for the damnedest creatures. He wondered about the old man. And where the little girl had come from if Gwen had never had a husband.

Never having a husband didn't mean she'd never partaken of the pleasures of the marital bed. He'd never married, thanks to Marian, but he'd pleasured his share of women in his time.

Jake wondered if Gwen's skin was as soft as her heart. He moved restlessly in the bed. He shouldn't be thinking those kinds of thoughts. Michaels didn't act without a purpose. And one thing Jake was pretty sure about, Michaels hadn't sent Jake here to sleep with a woman.

Soon enough Jake would figure out exactly why he'd been sent here. Until then, he had no intention of doing anything to annoy Michaels. Jake's last trip, Michaels had said. Jake punched down his pillow. No mossy green eyes were going to keep him from finding the peace which had eluded him for over a hundred years.

Gwen stood on the porch fronting the oldest section of the main house and surveyed her domain. Home. How she'd envied Bert the steadfast pioneer genes running through his blood. No rootless wandering and always pulling up stakes for the Winthrop family. Bless Bert for giving her his home and his family history. She hugged herself. Her own home. A place to raise Crissie, a place where they could put down roots. Dynamite couldn't blast her from her home.

From the other side of the screen door behind her she could hear Mrs. Kent, Doris, rattling pans in the kitchen. When Gwen counted her blessings, she put Bert's house-keeper first. Nothing disturbed the forty-six-year-old widow, and Doris cooked like a dream. Crissie adored her. So did Gwen. Typically, Doris had taken Mack in her stride.

Down the road some horses grazed in the pasture. The cows were pastured further from the house. Gwen knew less than nothing of cows and horses, but she could learn. Like any other business, the most important thing was to hire good employees.

Employees like Jakob Stoner.

Her gaze sharpened as the ranch pickup came into view down the road. Jake. He'd think she was watching for him. She wasn't. She'd almost forgotten he'd left hours earlier to check fences and stock. She had a lot more on her mind than the cowboy who'd come so for-tuitously into her life yesterday.

He'd told her last night over dinner what he'd planned for today. This morning Doris had found his breakfast dishes rinsed and stacked neatly beside the sink. Jake Stoner started the day early.

Gwen squinted into the sun. Two people sat in the pickup. Jake had a passenger. Someone to see her?

Or to see Jake? A friend, maybe. A girlfriend. Gwen narrowed her eyes in speculation. Or a wife. Jake hadn't volunteered much about himself, and for some reason, she'd hesitated to ask. Hesitated to ask questions she wouldn't have had a second thought about asking up in Denver. Getting-to-know-you questions. Somehow, here, they seemed prying questions. Or maybe, it wasn't here. Maybe it was Jake. A self-contained aura surrounded him, making him complete within himself. As if he needed no one. Wanted no one.

In any case, she wasn't interested in his personal life. Only in his ranching skills.

She'd never considered he might have a wife. Or a family. He needed to learn he couldn't move a wife and a couple of kids onto her place without checking first with her. He seemed to think because he knew more about ranching than she did, he could do whatever he wanted.

That was her fault. She'd been too polite, wording her orders as requests. Not because he made her nervous or she was afraid or reluctant to give him orders. She'd never been the type to boss people around. Issuing curt orders wasn't her style. He recognized she was the employer and he the employee.

That the situation amused him was only conjecture on her part.

And Lawrence had vouched for him. Well, not exactly for Jake, whom he'd never met. At Gwen's request Jake had talked to Lawrence on the phone, and later Lawrence had allowed as how Jake seemed to know the cattle business. Lawrence had been Bert's trusted right-hand man for years, and he ought to know.

The pickup passed between the huge stone pillars at the far edge of the ranch yard and pulled up by the house. Jake acknowledged Gwen's presence with a slight smile. Unless he was smiling at the house which amused him so much. No matter what anyone else thought, she liked the way the two additions, one rustic log and one Queen Anne Victorian, reflected the eras and tastes of the builders. The house, like the Winthrops, had grown and settled into the land.

Jake stepped from the truck. His boots raised slight clouds of dust. "Hi. Where's my little pardner?"

"Taking a nap." He'd shaved. He looked less disreputable, but no less dangerous. Gwen couldn't rid herself of the notion that Jake Stoner looked exactly as an outlaw from the Old West must have looked. An air of watchfulness about him forcibly reminded her of the way wild animals in documentaries scented the wind for danger. Jake turned, speaking across the pickup to his passenger, and Gwen studied his profile. His jaw was strong, the kind that proclaimed its owner a determined man, a man not to be trifled with.

Not that she wanted to trifle with him. Idly she wondered if any woman had ever caressed his jaw in an attempt to soften it. Now what put that stupid thought in her head? The answer came to her immediately. She'd been reading one of Bert's family journals. One started in 1911 by a young woman as she'd set out on the train from Chicago to meet her sweetheart in Colorado. The woman's romantic nonsense had seeped into Gwen's brain.

"Someone to see you," Jake said.

The wrinkled old man who climbed down from the truck turned intense brown eyes on her. "You the gal Bert left his place to?"

"Yes. I'm Gwen Ashton."

The man cackled with laughter. "Bert leaving his place to a purdy little gal he barely knew shure set some people back on their heels. Specially that no-account nephew of Bert's. Serves him right. Counting his chickens afore they was hatched."

Gwen had had it with people speculating about Bert's motives. "I wasn't his mistress and he wasn't my sugar daddy," she snapped.

"Never said ya was. Bert was plenty tickled he found somebody who'd love the place the way he done. He thought about leaving it to Lawrence, but said Lawrence had the look a death on him." The man spat on the ground. "Don't know how Bert knew. Heard Lawrence's up in Denver in the hospital with cancer eating away his guts. He'll be ridin' the range with Bert purdy soon."

Leaning against the front of the pickup, his arms crossed over his chest, Jake gave Gwen a thoughtful look. She knew he'd taken the job on a temporary basis only. Crossing her fingers where Jake couldn't see them, she said quickly, "Lawrence, Mr. Hingle, is being treated." His daughter told Gwen the cancer had advanced beyond help. "I'm sure he'll be fine." It wasn't exactly a lie. Miracles happened.

"He won't be back," the old man said with finality before spitting again. "Heard ya need help, so I come over. Name's Tom. Where do I bunk?"

Gwen opened her mouth and closed it again, struck dumb. The man was older than dirt, and if he stood one inch over five feet tall, she'd be amazed. Her eyes swung to Jake. He gazed blandly back. The old man wasn't his problem.

"Uh, well, Tom, as you can see, I've already hired Mr. Stoner. While I appreciate your—"

"I hear tell Rod Heath done gone to Cheyenne." The big lump in his cheek moved up and down with his words. "Not gonna hire him again when he comes crawling back, are ya?"

"No, that is..." She wanted to bite her tongue. She should have lied.

"Thought not. You look too salty for that."

Gwen ignored the smothered choke of laughter from the direction of the pickup. She wondered how funny Jake would find it if she hired Tom as his assistant. Of course, she couldn't hire a man of his age. Not for the kind of physical labor needed on a ranch. "I appreciate you taking the time and trouble to come way out here, but I'm not hiring another hand at present. Mr. Stoner will give you a ride back into town." That didn't sound too hospitable. "Would you care for a glass of iced tea before you leave?"

The man moved the lump to the other side of his jaw, giving her close study throughout the operation. "Ain't you some kind a fancy numbers lady?"

So much for being a Certified Public Accountant. "I'm a CPA, yes."

"Then ya otter be able to count. You had two ranch hands, now ya got one. You need anuther."

"Uh, well, it might look that way, but, the thing is, it's pretty slow around here right now. We don't need to replace Rod for a while."

"Slow. In August?" The man snorted. "She don't know a damn thing about ranching, does she?" He directed the question to Jake who merely smiled.

Gwen gave the tall cowboy a look of entreaty. He could chime in anytime.

"Yeah, boss lady?"

She didn't believe that artless look for one second. He was reminding her it was her ranch. Fine. She'd handled personnel matters before. She'd deal with this one. Firmly she said, "Thank you for applying for the job, Mr., uh, Tom. If we find we need help, we'll certainly keep you in mind."

The man gave her a disgusted look. "Yur jes like that young whippersnapper son of mine. Thinking I'm too old to do anything but set in a rocking chair. I aint dead yet." He spit again before squinting up at Gwen. "Maybe I caint keep up with this young feller—" he nodded at Jake "—but you aint seen the day I caint outwork that no-account Rod you had. I'm of a mind to sue you for age discrimination.''

The old man had one foot in the grave, and he was threatening to sue her. Pure bravado. They both knew, even if he did sue her, he'd never win. He stared up at her with a proud, pugnacious look which almost hid the resignation in his eyes. He felt discarded before his time. Gwen sighed inwardly. Surely Jake could find something easy for the man to do. ''All right,'' she said, ''I'll hire you.'' She couldn't let him think she was hiring him out of pity. ''I can't afford to be sued, but I'm not a charity. I'm hiring you under the same conditions I hired Jake. A month's trial period.''

Tom proudly adjusted a beat-up brown cowboy hat over his few strands of hair. ''Ya won't be sorry, Ma'am. Ya just done got yourself a top hand.'' He hesitated, then a crafty expression narrowed his eyes. ''Name's Smith. Tom Smith.'' The look on his face dared her to challenge the blatantly obvious lie.

Gwen only hoped he didn't kill himself before the month was up. ''Tom,'' she called as he headed back to the pickup for his gear, ''can I ask you one thing?''

''You can ask,'' the old man said cautiously. ''Mebbe I'll answer and mebbe I won't.''

''Just how old is your son?''

''Damn fool kid's still wet behind the ears.'' Tom spit at the truck's front wheel. ''Sixty-two last birthday. You let that be,'' he snapped at Jake who'd reached into the back of the pickup. ''I carry my own rig. Just point me.''

Jake pointed to the small stone house. ''Bunk in any bedroom but mine.''

Gwen watched him disappear into the employees' quarters, then turned on Jake. ''I don't want to hear one word from you about me hiring him. I don't care if he does slow you down. I don't care if you do have to invent work for him. I'm the boss around here and I say he stays.''

''All right.''

''What does that mean?'' she asked suspiciously.

He ambled over to the base of the porch steps, and shoved his hat to the back of his head. ''It means you're the boss.''

''Yes, I am the boss. And don't you forget it.''

''Ma'am, a man's not likely to forget anything about you.'' One easy step with those long legs of his and he stood on the porch in front of Gwen. He gently touched her cheek with a glove-clad finger. ''Tom was right about you.''

''I know, I don't know anything about ranching.'' Or outlaws, she thought nonsensically.

He shook his head, a faint smile on his lips. ''About you being a 'purdy little gal.' You stir a man's insides.'' He backed her up against the stone porch pillar and tipped up her chin, his gaze settling on her mouth.

''I don't want you to kiss me.''

''No, Ma'am.'' He smiled, barely showing white, even teeth.

''You're my employee,'' she said stiffly.

His smile widened. ''If you mean your cowhand, yes I am, boss lady.''

''I don't believe in mixing business and pleasure.''

He laughed, deep in the back of his throat. ''You're right about that, Ma'am. Kissing you will be pure pleasure.''

She'd never been kissed by an outlaw. She didn't intend to let one kiss her now. ''You're not still planning to kiss me?''

''Yes, ma'am.''

She ought to fire him. Maybe she should kiss him first. Out of curiosity. Then she'd fire him. Except she needed him. Even with Tom, she couldn't operate the ranch alone. So she couldn't kiss him. Because she couldn't fire him.

She'd deliberated too long. He lowered his head. She expected a hard, forceful kiss to demonstrate his masculine superiority. His mouth settled gently on hers, a whisper of a kiss. He nibbled on her lips, tiny bites as if tasting her. Tingling little bites he slowly bathed with his warm, moist tongue. Which did nothing to calm the tingling. Nearby a grasshopper whirred. Cows mooed in the distance. If he'd panted and grabbed at her clothes, Gwen would have fought him off. His steady breathing gave her the courage to indulge a certain intellectual curiosity. She'd stop in a minute.

The gentle persuasion of his lips told her he wanted her to open her mouth. No wonder all those prim schoolteachers used to run off with outlaws, she thought an instant later. Cowboys, outlaws, knew how to kiss.

Lightly she touched his cheek. He'd shaved his heavy growth of beard, but that had been hours ago and fresh stubble rasped against her fingertips. She slid her hands down his neck, across his shoulders. His strength seemed to flow through his soft, weathered cotton shirt into her fingers. She tightened her grip, enjoying the flexing of his hard muscles.

He took away his mouth and stepped back. Her eyes shot open in protest. He gave her a lazy smile as he lifted his hand, caught a gloved finger between his teeth and yanked off the glove. Dropping it, he ran his fingers over the side of her face and closed the distance between them. A light breeze danced by, carrying a hint of dust and the smell of sage. Gwen pushed off his hat and threaded her fingers through his thick shaggy hair. She'd stop kissing him in a minute.

Sandwiched between his large, hard body and the sunwarmed stone pillar, her body molded itself to his hard thighs, the large belt buckle at his waist, his broad shoulders. Work-roughened fingers ran lightly over her jaw-line, trailed down her neck, and traced the neckline of her shirt.

The feel of a button slipping free brought Gwen to her senses. She stiffened and drew back, fighting for composure. And the courage to look him in the eye. What could she possibly have been thinking of? The man worked for her. She didn't want him kissing her. She didn't want the heat from his body coiling around her. If he made one arrogant, gloating, what-a-big-boy-am-I remark, she'd smack him.

A tanned finger lightly skimmed the tip of a breast straining against the fabric of her shirt. "Maybe I should have expected that."

Gwen's head snapped up even as she slapped aside his hand. "Expected what?" she demanded fiercely. "That I'd be an easy touch?"

"I wasn't thinking about that, but since you ask, Ma'am, you are definitely an easy touch. I knew that even without the old man."

His slow smile warmed her all the way to her toes. Or would have. If she wasn't already boiling mad. Jabbing her finger into Jake's chest, she forced him to retreat, yelling, "I was not Bert's mistress." She curled her fingers into a fist and followed Jake down the porch steps, pounding him in time with her angry words. "I did not manipulate him with sex. I did not sleep with Bert and I'm not going to sleep with you."

Jake abruptly halted, brushing her fist aside as one brushed off a fly. "Who's talking about Bert? I'm talking about Tom."

"Tom!" Gwen screeched. "You think I'm sleeping with Tom?" She hauled back her right arm to slug him.

Effortlessly Jake captured her arm. "What's wrong with you? I'm talking about you taking in Tom, like you took in Mack."

Gwen froze, her left arm halted mid-swing. "You're talking about me hiring Tom?"

"Sure. What the hell were you talking about?"

"Nothing. Never mind. Let go of me." She concentrated on brushing off her sleeve where he'd gripped her arm. "I'm a little sensitive about inheriting Bert's property. His nephew Gordon has made a number of unsavory accusations."

"Tom says he's a no-account. No one's going to pay any attention to his sour grapes."

"About Tom." She concentrated on the tanned skin in the vee of Jake's shirt. "I know he's old, but—" A finger pressed against her mouth stopped her.

"Tom's going to work out just fine."

"That's sweet of you to say, but—"

"Honey, I haven't been sweet since my ma weaned me."

She decided to overlook what he'd called her. His drawl hinted of the South. She had the impression down there everyone called everyone "honey." The issue here was Tom. "I'm glad you have no objection to my hiring him. I'm confident you can find something for him to do that won't be beyond his capabilities."

"Tom knows more about cows and horses than I'll ever know."

"Tom?"

"He's a horse doctor, a veterinarian. Took his son and then his grandson into his practice, and they nudged him out. Thinking they were doing him a favor. Didn't want him dropping dead in the office."

"How do you know that?"

"Tom'd thumbed a ride with somebody partway here. I picked him up and brought him the rest of the way. We got to talking and he told me all about it."

"And you believed him? He doesn't talk like any veterinarian I've ever met."

Jake chuckled. "Tom thought a city lady would be more likely to hire him if she thought he'd add a little local color. I could have told him that wasn't necessary."

"You should have told me who he was."

Jake shrugged. "What difference would it have made? You'd still have hired him."

Unwilling to argue the point, she switched tactics. "I expect the people who work for me to keep me informed. Is that clear, Mr. Stoner?"

"Sure, boss," he said easily. "Didn't I just tell you about Tom? I know you hired him because you felt sorry for him, but forget that. If you're serious about this ranching business—"

"I'm serious."

"Tom can teach you about the livestock."

"That's what I'm paying you for."

A grasshopper landed near Jake's boot. "Knowing about cows and horses and caring for the land takes a heap of studying on. You'll need Tom when I'm gone." He ground the insect under his toe. "I'm just passing through."

"Jake, it's none of my business, but... A man like you could do anything he put his mind to. Why don't you settle down?"

He picked his hat up from the ground and carefully brushed the dust from it. "No, Ma'am, it's not your business," he finally said. "Besides, there's no way to explain it. Settling down's something I can't do. I have to move on when I'm not needed anymore."

"Who decides when you're not needed? You? Like you decided about kissing me?"

He gave her a long look. "You telling me you didn't want me to kiss you?"

"The question was, are you the one who decides you're not needed anymore?"

"No."

"All right, then. As long as we both understand how it is."

"I understand. I doubt you do." He settled his hat on his head. "One other thing, boss lady, be mighty careful about laying down the law around here, and saying what you will and won't do, unless you're damned sure you can back up your words."

"That sounds very much like a threat," Gwen said slowly. "I'm not sure why. I'm not so stupid I'd hire an expert on ranching and then disregard his advice."

Cool gray eyes rested on her face. "Then take this advice, boss lady. Don't be issuing any ultimatums about whether or not you'll sleep with me. If I decide to sleep with you, I will." A lazy smile crawled over his face. "And, honey, you'll want me in your bed." He turned and headed toward the pickup, sweeping his glove from the ground in passing.

He had the truck door open by the time Gwen found her voice. "You're fired!"

He looked at her through the open window. "You can't fire me." The pickup engine roared to life, and Jake backed the truck away from the house.

"And don't call me honey!"

The truck backfired, then bounced noisily around to the barn.

"I thought there was more in the air last night at the dinner table than the smell of roast beef."

Gwen looked over her shoulder at the housekeeper. "Maybe you smelled the carrots."

Doris laughed, wiping her hands on her apron as she walked out on the porch. "It appears to me Crissie isn't the only one with a crush on our handsome cowboy."

"Have you been at the cooking sherry? You've obviously been eavesdropping, so you know he kissed me. It wasn't my idea, and he won't be kissing me again."

"I think he will if he wants to."

"I don't care what he wants." Clasping her hands around a porch pillar, Gwen swayed back. "I don't want him kissing me."

"Why not?"

"He's not my type."

"That man is any woman's type. Don't tell me you haven't thought about having a sexy hunk like him in your bed."

"I'm not interested in sexy hunks. I want to put down roots for Crissie and me. I want to keep this ranch from going under. If and when I decide to get married, I want a stable, dependable man who's willing to settle down here and create a home and family with me."

Doris moved to gently massage Gwen's spine. "You've weathered a lot of changes in the past year. Your brother and his wife being killed in that car accident, you taking in Crissie, Bert dying and leaving you his place. You quit your job, moved down here and barely got settled before Lawrence got ill and Rod quit. You're reading all hours of the night trying to cram your head full of ranching know-how, sorting Bert's papers for Prudence, trying to make a home for you and Crissie and make a go of the ranch. You need a little fun, Gwen. Jake claims he'll be moving on. Nothing says you can't play around a little with him until he does."

"Doris Kent. Are you advising me to have an affair?"

"He's a good-looking male. You're a single female. Do the math, Gwen. You're the CPA."

"You're a single female. You sleep with him," Gwen retorted.

"I would. If he looked at me like he looks at you."

Gwen couldn't care less how Jake Stoner looked at her. Even if Doris was dying to tell her. Which she must be, or she wouldn't have brought it up. Gwen certainly couldn't tell the older woman to shut up. The silence stretched out. "Well?" Gwen finally demanded. "How does he look at me?"

"The same way Mack looked at that roast last night as I carved it for dinner. Like he was starving to death."

CHAPTER THREE

JAKE tossed and turned in his bed as snores reverberated down the hall. If they were on a trail drive, the cattle would have stampeded halfway back to Texas by now. Jake didn't know how a man as little as Tom could make that much noise. No wonder a body couldn't sleep.

All the inventions they'd come up with in this century, you'd think they could stop a man from snoring. Gwen's car even had buttons to lock the doors and open and shut the windows. The next time Jake came back, he'd remember that. Funny how he couldn't recall the events and the people who'd brought him back, but knowledge soaked in and lay dormant until the time came when he needed it. He knew how to drive Bert's thirty-year-old pickup. He knew about television, although the last time he'd seen it, the picture had been in black and white—and they sure didn't show all those advertisements for things women never used to talk about in front of men. He couldn't imagine what he'd see the next time he came back.

Except Michaels had promised this was the last time.

Michaels. Damn the man, or whatever he was. Jake could appreciate a good shenanigan as well as the next man, and being returned to his own house sort of tickled his funny bone, but doggone it, then Michaels had gone too far. Taking a man who hadn't lain with a woman for over one hundred years and plunking him down with a boss lady like Gwen.

Jake stared grimly at the ceiling. For a plugged nickel, he'd pull his freight. Except he couldn't.

A man like him shouldn't have calico fever, and he

had it in a bad way. He wanted a woman. Not any
woman. Gwen. He wanted her under him, those green
eyes begging him to bury himself in her. Michaels
wasn't here. He'd never know if Jake took her. Jake
snorted. He had a feeling Michaels knew everything.

After Jake finished building his place—this place,
he'd planned to marry Marian. Then Ma's letter had
come. He and Marian had argued about whether Jake
was obligated. Marian had demanded he choose between
her and Luther, then thrown a fit at the guarded look
she'd seen in Jake's eyes. Before he said, she knew he'd
be going after his little brother. Luther had appreciated
Jake's doing his duty as little as Marian did. Jake smiled
cynically. Marian had changed her mind quick enough
after meeting Luther when Jake had brought his brother
to the ranch. Later, Marian was the one insisting Jake
do his duty and go after Luther.

Jake had a feeling Michaels hadn't thought much of
the way Jake did his duty. When Jake looked into
Michael's eyes, he saw the judgment. And his own sins.

He'd been decent enough to deny himself Marian's
body, telling himself he could wait until they were wed.
Someone—fate?—owed Jake a woman. An intriguing
thought hit him. Maybe Michaels wasn't such a bad guy.
Maybe he'd sent Jake on this particular job to give Jake
his last shot at a woman. Where Jake was headed, maybe
men didn't lay with women.

If Jake was going to have only one more opportunity
to sleep with a woman, he didn't mind one bit if that
woman was Gwen. Those eyes of hers switched shades
of green with every thought. He wondered how it was a
handsome woman like her hadn't harnessed some man
by now. When it came to men she was barely green-
broke. Willing to kiss, but skittish.

Jake folded his hands behind his head. Gwen had gotten all riled up after that kiss, but not because he'd kissed

her. Because she'd liked him kissing her. And that, she hadn't liked. He laughed softly. He could kiss Gwen all he wanted, and there wasn't a thing she could do about it. Jake would go when Michaels decided he'd go. And not before.

Maybe next time Jake wouldn't stop with just a kiss. She'd like that, too. Just because he'd lived over a hundred years ago, didn't mean Jake didn't know a thing or two about pleasing women.

Jake waited until Doris took Crissie to the kitchen to clean up before he sat back in his chair and pushed aside his dinner plate. "Can you ride?"

Despite Doris's astounding observation this afternoon, Gwen had no intention of crawling into bed with Jake Stoner. She ought to fire him, but unfortunately, she needed him. Tom whatever-his-name-was might be a retired veterinarian, but she doubted very much if he was up to the physical demands of the ranch. She needed Jake's muscles. But that's all she needed. A fact she planned to make perfectly clear to Jake Stoner. She employed him. Nothing more.

Accordingly, Gwen had avoided all speech with him at the dinner table. Doris obviously knew Tom and the circumstances of his hiring, and the two of them, along with Crissie, had done the talking. Gwen wished she had the nerve to insist Jake and Tom eat in the kitchen, but she knew Doris wouldn't take kindly to the idea. Bert had fed his hands in the family dining room. As long as Doris did the cooking, the hands would eat in the dining room.

Jake was waiting for her answer. "I've ridden a few times," she said. "Mostly when I came down to visit Bert. I've been meaning to ride more, but Lawrence always took me in the pickup."

"Which horse?"

"Susie, named for Susan Magoffin. Bert named all his horses after historical sites or people related to this area." Gwen warmed to her topic. "There's Willy, after William Bent from Bent's Fort, and Kearny for Colonel Stephen Kearny who led the Army of the West, and Cimarron for the river, and Vegas for Las Vegas, New Mexico, not Nevada, and—"

"Which one's Susie?"

"The tan one," Gwen said coolly. Jake might not share her enthusiasm for local history, but he didn't need to be rude. "Bert called her a buckskin."

"So you can't ride," Jake said in disgust. "If you could, he wouldn't have put you on that old nag."

"She's not a nag. She's perfectly sweet."

"She's so old if you fired a six-shooter behind her, she'd barely switch her tail." He sighed heavily. "There's no help for it. Be at the corral by the barn after breakfast."

"I plan to spend the morning going over Bert's books."

"Change of plans. The corral after breakfast."

"That sounds like an order, Mr. Stoner," Gwen said tightly.

"Good. I wouldn't want you to think you have a choice in the matter." He smiled lazily across the table.

"Now see here, Mr. Stoner, I will not—"

"What? Succeed? Learn? Become a rancher?"

"I will not be ordered around by someone who works for me."

"Do you know when to move the cows?" he asked.

"I'm sure Bert wrote it down somewhere."

He gave her a pitying look. "You don't know. Do you know the difference between noxious weeds and good grass? And I don't mean that stuff that grows in town. Do you know if the stock ponds are filling okay?

If the calves are getting enough milk? When to wean them? Which bull to put to which cows?''

"I'm a CPA, not a rancher. I hired you and Tom to tell me those things.''

"Honey, you were a CPA. Now you're either a rancher or a squatter who doesn't know a damn thing about livestock or the land and who'll go belly-up.''

"I don't see how—''

"You will by the time I get through. Tomorrow morning. At the corral.'' Jake pushed back his chair and stood up. "If you're a good girl and do what you're told, maybe I'll let you play boss the rest of the day.'' He strolled out of the room.

A slight choking sound broke the silence. Gwen turned on Tom who was hiding the lower half of his face in his napkin. "You think that's funny? Wait until he tries to run your life.''

"Don't come across many like him anymore. All rawhide and iron,'' Tom said, his voice filled with admiration.

"All bully and blowhard.''

"The man's right, you know. You need to learn if you're going to keep this place going. He'll make a good instructor. I watched him this afternoon. He's patient, thorough, even-tempered, and careful. Jake's not one to rush heedlessly into a situation without checking things out, and he's steady. It'd take a lot to disturb his equilibrium.''

"Equilibrium is a pretty big word for you, isn't it? What happened to words like purdy and aint?''

"Jake told me he disclosed my little secret.''

"After the fact.'' Another example of him thinking he knew better than anyone else. "And I wouldn't exactly call Jake Stoner overly cautious.''

"I didn't say overly cautious. The man knows his

worth, I'll grant him that. Some might even make the mistake of thinking he's on the arrogant side.''

"Thinking that is no mistake. He's a cocky, presumptuous, arrogant, overconfident male who suffers from excessive testosterone.''

Tom chuckled. "You're not talking about his ranching abilities. You're talking about him kissing you this afternoon.''

Gwen sprang to her feet. "Was the whole world watching? I was not talking about a stupid kiss. I'd forgotten all about it.''

Gwen walked slowly toward the corral by the barn. She wanted to ride a horse. Jake's order had nothing to do with her decision. She wouldn't even allow him to ride with her. She'd tell him to saddle up Susie, and then she'd order him to—to do something. Something out of her presence. Something to remind him who was boss.

A mud-colored horse with white down its nose threw up its head and watched Gwen walk toward the corral where the horse was penned. The buckskin mare grazed on the other side of the pasture.

Jake Stoner leaned back against the corral fence, his elbows resting on the top rail, one boot hooked over the bottom rail. "Shouldn't have slept half the day away. It's going to be hot.''

"Do you practice being obnoxious, Mr. Stoner, or does it come naturally?''

"Call me Jake, honey.''

"I'm going to call you unemployed, if you don't quit calling me honey. My name is Gwen.''

"With that honey-colored hair, I think you'd be used to men calling you honey.''

"My hair is ash blond, but men don't call me ashes,'' she snapped. "Now call Susie over so I can ride.''

He nodded over his shoulder. "He's an eight-year-old

gelding. Mostly quarter horse. Some Arabian. Your friend Bert knew what he was doing when he trained horses. You've got some good, well-trained ones. I think you and this horse will work well together. He's not too spooky for a beginning rider, but enough of a horse to challenge you.''

"I'm not riding Vegas. I prefer to ride Susie," Gwen said firmly.

"Sure, riding her once in a while won't hurt. Today you're working with him, Vegas, if that's his name.''

"It's his name, and I'm riding Susie today. Right now.''

Still leaning against the corral, Jake shrugged his shoulders and crossed his arms over his chest. "Okay.''

Gwen tapped her foot. "Well? I'm waiting.''

"What for? If you want to ride the mare, go ahead.''

"I would like her saddled.''

He nodded to his right. "There's a saddle.''

Gwen silently counted to ten. "I want you to call Susie over here and I want you to saddle her for me.''

"Nope.''

"What do you mean, nope? You can't refuse. I gave you an order.''

"You're sure a great one for giving orders, aren't you?''

"You listen to me, Mr. Stoner. This is my ranch, my land, my horses, and my saddles. I own them, and you work for me. When I tell you to saddle me a horse, I expect that horse to be saddled.''

"The Indians used to say a man couldn't own the land. I'm not sure you can own a horse, either. If a horse trusts you and wants to work with you, he will. If he doesn't, he won't.''

"Then, Mr. Stoner, I'll fire the horse just like I'm firing you.''

"Honey, when are you going to get it through that pretty head of yours, you can't fire me?"

"Don't call me honey and I certainly can fire you."

"Don't call me Mr. Stoner, and you can't fire me because you need me, or I wouldn't be here. And as soon as you quit acting like a spoiled little brat, and admit you're scared spitless, we might get somewhere."

"I am not afraid of horses."

"I didn't say you were. Most ranchers were born and raised to it. You don't know a cow from a heifer. You'd be an idiot if you weren't scared about pulling up stakes and bringing your little girl down here to start a new life. I'd be terrified if I had to walk into some fancy office up in Denver, sit down at a desk, and pretend I knew about taxes. I also know I'd have to learn. Like you have to learn." He paused before adding in a flat voice, "If you're going to be stubborn and deny your ignorance and refuse to learn, tell me now. I'm not wasting time or energy on a gutless greenhorn."

Gwen moved over to the corral fence and grabbed the top bar with her hands, then leaned back the length of her arms. "Why don't you say what you're really thinking? What everybody around here thinks. That I'm an idiot for leaving a perfectly good, high-paying job for some fantasy which exists only in Hollywood. You think I have no more business out here on a ranch than that horse would have trying to tap dance on Broadway." She pulled herself up to the fence and pushed back again. "You think I bought these stupid cowgirl clothes and moved out here in the middle of nowhere and I don't have a clue what to do."

Gwen kicked at the dirt with the toe of her boot. "Well, you're right. I don't have a clue, but I'm not stupid. I intend to learn. Crissie is going to have what I never had—a stable childhood, roots."

"A white picket fence," he said with sarcasm. "I

don't see what's so stable about leaving a high-paying job for the uncertainties of ranching.''

She owed him no explanation, but she gave one anyway. ''I've always been good with numbers, so going into accounting was a logical move for me. There will always be taxes, which means stable employment. It's long hours of computer time and paperwork, but I didn't mind until I had Crissie. During the height of tax season I worked from seven in the morning until ten or eleven at night. That's no way to bring up a child. I knew I had to quit the accounting firm, but I didn't know what I'd do. Then Bert died and left me his ranch. Here, even if I have to keep long hours, I'll have Crissie at my side. That's important to me. And best for her.'' Gwen dug her fingernails into the wooden railing. ''I'm not quitting here. I'm not running back to Denver with my tail between my legs. I'm here, and I'm going to stay here. I'm never leaving.''

''You'll leave. You'll get tired of the mud and the dirt and the bugs and the hard work and long hours and the loneliness. Tired of pulling calves and doctoring horses and feeding in winter. You'll miss your restaurants and stores and movie theaters. You'll get tired of playing cowgirl and run back to the city where you belong.''

Gwen flung up her head. ''I belong here. Since you obviously don't think so, you're the one who doesn't belong. I know I have a lot to learn, but I'll find someone to help me who doesn't spend all his time trying to chase me away. Pack up your things and get out.''

''Honey, you're as single-minded as a thirsty cow who smells the Pecos River after being driven eighty miles without water. I told you, I'll leave when it's time.''

''Maybe you don't hear so good, buddy. Ms. Ashton asked you to leave now. Hit the road.''

Gwen whirled. ''Gordon. I didn't hear you drive up.''

The burly, brown-haired man in his thirties smirked at her before pointing a thumb toward Jake. "Who's the jerk? What happened to Rod?"

"Rod quit. This is my new—uh—foreman. Jake, this is Gordon Pease, Bert's nephew."

"Jake Stoner," Jake said. Neither man extended his hand.

Gordon put his hands in his pants' pockets and rocked back on his heels. "I couldn't help but hear some of what he said, Gwen. I think Uncle Bert was going around the bend, if you know what I mean, dumping this place on you."

"If you'd bothered to visit him occasionally, you'd have known Bert was not the least bit senile," Gwen said.

"Yeah, maybe I should have visited more. That would have put quite a crimp in your plans to take him for all he was worth, wouldn't it?"

"What do you want, Gordon?" Gwen asked coldly.

"What I've always wanted. What's due me. You know you're in over your head here. You'll lose the place to the bank in a year or two. Sell to me now and I'll give you enough to get you and the kid back to Denver. Uncle Bert bragged what a great CPA you are. You won't have no trouble finding another job. We can go in the house right now and write out the paperwork."

"You know as well as I do the estate isn't settled until it's gone through probate. Even if I wanted to sell to you, which I don't, I couldn't." Gwen gave Gordon a fixed smile. "Thank you for stopping by to see how I'm doing. Now, if that's all, I have work to do."

Gordon's eyes narrowed to black slits. "You think you've won, Ms. Ashton, but I ain't through yet. By rights, this place belongs to me." Turning, he stomped off around the barn.

Gwen followed him to make sure he got in his car

and drove away. Jake trailed behind her. Passing the corner of the barn, she saw the front of the house where Crissie and Mack sat on the porch steps. Crissie waved shyly to Gordon. Gwen couldn't hear the man's response, but Crissie's smile vanished, and Mack stood up and walked stiff-legged down the steps. Even from a distance, Gwen could see the raised hair on the back of the dog's neck. Gwen's heart skipped a beat, and she broke into a lope. Swearing fluently, Jake passed her. Gordon practically ran the last few steps to his dark green pickup and yanked open the door.

The crisis, if one had existed other than in Gwen's mind, was averted. She slowed. Gordon kicked the side of the oncoming dog, and Mack yelped in pain. Crissie screamed and scrambled down the steps toward the dog. Terrified the injured dog would bite Crissie, Gwen ran toward her niece, cursing legs which refused to obey her demand for speed.

Gordon jumped in the truck, started it, backed up, then moved forward. Heading straight for the dog. And Crissie. Surely he'd see Crissie and stop. Gwen screamed at him and pumped her legs harder. She couldn't get there in time. Crissie stood frozen, a look of horror on her face as she saw the truck bearing down on her. Gwen screamed at Gordon again. Jake dashed in front of the pickup, scooped up Crissie, shoved the dog out of the truck's path, and jumped aside. Gordon honked his horn, made an obscene gesture at Gwen, fishtailed the pickup through a U-turn and tore out of the yard, an angry column of dust in his wake.

Forcing her trembling legs forward, Gwen made it to the porch before she collapsed.

"He's a bad man. He hurt Mack."

"Are you okay?" Gwen grabbed Crissie and hugged her tightly.

The little girl wiggled free. "I have to see Mack. He's hurt."

"Mack's okay." Jake dropped to the porch steps beside Gwen. "Just a little bruise where the bad man kicked him, but I don't think anything's broken. Tom can look him over when he gets back."

Crissie stooped and kissed Mack's side, then straightened to say, "I don't like the bad man."

"Neither do I, pardner, neither do I."

Gwen clenched her knees, fighting for control. "He wouldn't have stopped. Maybe he didn't see her or understand what I was yelling, I don't know. But if it hadn't been for you…" Her fingernails dug into her kneecaps. A little over a year ago Dan and Monica had died a block from Gwen's Denver apartment. The flashing lights, shouting voices, and the smell of burned rubber haunted her dreams.

Crissie returned to climb onto Gwen's lap. "Are you hurt?"

Clutching the child thankfully, Gwen shoved aside the agonizing memories. The living needed her now. Crissie needed reassurance. "No, sweetie, I'm okay." She paused, her voice caught in her throat.

"You're crying." Crissie patted Gwen's wet cheek. "Don't cry. I kiss you well."

Gwen took a deep breath and inhaled the comforting scents of orange juice and baby shampoo. "I'm not crying. Just winded from running. I'll be okay as soon as I catch my breath." She squeezed the child on her lap. If she let go of Crissie, her niece might fly apart into a million pieces. Or she would. "He could have hit her," Gwen said numbly. "How could he not see her?"

"Whatever made Bert think you could handle the ranch?" Jake asked in disgust, leaning back on his elbows. "Do you go to pieces at every little thing? Maybe you figure I'll feel sorry for you and excuse you from work today. I won't.''

Gwen slowly raised her head to stare at him in disbelief. "Are you really that cruel and hard?"

"Look at it this way, honey. It's me if you want to keep the ranch, or him if you don't." His cool gaze flaunted a challenge.

After a moment, Gwen carefully stood up and set Crissie on the ground. Thankfully her gelatinous bones didn't disgrace her. She looked Jake right in the eye. "I want one thing perfectly understood, Mr. Stoner. My bones may have turned to pudding at what just happened, but I am not a quitter. I'll never be the rancher Bert was, and okay, I'll never know as much about cows and stuff as you and Tom do, but I'm going to make it here. This is Crissie's and my home, and damn it, we're going to stay here."

"That's a bad word. You said a bad word."

Jake reached down and picked up Crissie. "You know what I think, pardner? If I kiss Gwen every time she says a bad word, I'll bet she'll quit saying them. What do you think?"

"Yes." Crissie clapped her hands together. "Kiss Gwen."

Gwen glared at Jake. "Don't you dare."

"Honey, you got six seconds to get your bohind down to that corral or I'll do more than kiss you."

Halfway to the corral, Gwen whirled around to glare at him. "All right. What is a bohind?"

Jake broke into laughter. "Let's put it this way, honey," he said between chuckles, "I've been following yours all the way down from the house, and you've got a mighty cute one."

Sniffing disdainfully, Gwen stuck her nose in the air and sailed down to the corral. Behind her she heard Crissie prattling to Jake, whose shoulders she rode. What

they were going to do with the child while they rode
horses, Gwen couldn't imagine.

Not that Jake had ever said anything about actually getting on a horse and riding. Gwen sank down onto the
old wooden bench on the porch, leaned against the
house, and stifled a groan. Hefting saddles on and off a
horse one or two million times used muscles CPAs
weren't often called upon to use. Her arms were undoubtedly twice as long as they'd been when she got up
this morning. At least Crissie had enjoyed the show from
her perch on the top corral railing next to Jake's broad
shoulders. Crissie sitting so far above the ground should
have made Gwen nervous, but oddly enough, it hadn't.
    Maybe it was like the Chinese. Hadn't she read they
believed if you saved someone's life, you were obligated
to take care of that person forever? Or was it the other
way around? Maybe Crissie was supposed to take care
of Jake. Gwen managed a halfhearted smile. Crissie
wouldn't mind that. The child had the worst case of hero
worship Gwen had ever seen. Crissie had monopolized
Jake at dinner, and talked of nothing else to her aunt
during her bath and bedtime preparations. She'd even
interrupted her bedtime story to chatter about Jake.
    Easy for Crissie to adore him. He hadn't made her
stand in that stupid corral not once, but twice today, for
hours on end, well, a long time, learning how to get a
horse to come to her, how to bridle and saddle him.
She'd patted Vegas and pushed him and picked up his
feet.... "Why would you call a part on a horse a frog?"
she asked the dark night.
    "When you're hoarse, why do you say you've got a
frog in your throat?" Jake pushed open the screen door
and came outside. He lowered himself to the bench beside her.
    She thought he'd returned to his quarters. "I wouldn't

say anything so stupid.'' Gwen slid as far from him as she could and still remain on the bench. She had to put some chairs on the porch. In the meantime, just because he was obnoxious and bossy and stubborn and a total pain in the neck didn't mean they couldn't share the bench. She could act like an adult. Maybe he'd learn something. ''And if I did, I wouldn't say it to you, because I'm not talking to you.''

''That's progress. At least you aren't firing me again.''

''I can't fire you, and you know it.''

''Sure I know it. I've been telling you that all along.''

''Whatever you've been ranting and raving about has nothing to do with anything. After you saved Crissie from what could have been a horrible...'' Gwen pressed her lips tightly together for a minute. ''Anyway, after this morning, I'm obligated to you. I should have thanked you then, but, well, I didn't, but I'm eternally grateful to you. I never could have reached Crissie in time.''

''About this morning.'' Jake clasped his hands around a knee and leaned back. ''I owe you an apology.''

''Yes, you do. You knew very well I wanted to go for a ride. Bert never made me do all that stuff. He let me get right on Susie and we rode all over the ranch.''

''You weren't riding,'' Jake said in disgust.

''I most certainly was. Ask Doris.''

''You were sitting on top of Susie. Just like you're sitting on this bench. Susie did what she wanted, and all you did was hang on. You were sight-seeing. Bert didn't mount you on one of his other horses, because he didn't want an inexperienced rider like you confusing them. A horse has to trust his rider. Susie trusted Bert. You were no different than a sack of flour to her.''

''Thank you very much,'' Gwen said sarcastically.

''Don't thank me yet. You've got a long way to go

before you can think like your horse. You have to know why he's twitching his ear, whipping his tail, and what he's thinking when he sees something on the trail in front of him. Every time he moves a muscle I want you to notice and anticipate what he's going to do. Horses aren't people or dogs or cats. They're horses and they think like horses.''

''Thank you for the fascinating zoology lesson. I came out here to enjoy a little solitude, and since that appears to be impossible, if you'll excuse me, I believe I'll go in.''

''No, I won't excuse you.''

''It was a rhetorical question which didn't require an answer,'' Gwen snapped.

''I'll leave as soon as I say my piece.''

Gwen had scooted to the extreme end of the bench, and when Jake stood, removing his balancing weight from the other end, his end of the bench shot up. Gwen's end shot down, dumping her to the floor. She landed hard. The bench landed on top of her.

''Are you okay?'' If Jake was concerned, he hid it well. He reached down to lift the bench off Gwen.

She'd had about all she wanted from this irritating, insufferable, obnoxious cowboy. She certainly didn't need his help. Jerking the bench away from him, she fended it in front on her like a shield. Or a weapon. ''Go away. And quit laughing. You did that on purpose.''

''I'm not laughing,'' he said in an amused voice. ''Pull in your horns, honey.''

''I'll give you horns.'' She jabbed the bench, legs first, at him.

Jake laughed and dodged out of the way. ''You're a rip-snorting terror, aren't you?''

In answer, Gwen rammed a bench leg into his thigh.

''Ouch, damn it. Give that to me before you hurt your-self.''

Gwen wrapped her arms around the wooden bench, hanging on to it with all her strength. "I don't take orders from you."

"You are the stubbornest woman." Jake pulled at the bench. "No wonder you're not hitched."

"Of all the sexist remarks." So mad she hardly knew what she was doing, Gwen let go of the bench.

At the same time, Jake gave a determined yank. Her lack of resistance caught him by surprise, and he took a hasty step backward on the narrow porch. His hindmost foot found nothing but air. He pitched backward off the low porch, the bench securely in his grip.

Gwen's brief moment of satisfaction fled in the face of total silence from beyond the porch. "Are you okay?" A slight breeze stirred a clump of tall grass. "Jake?" From inside the house came the faint sounds of the television program Doris watched. "Jake, quit playing games and answer me."

Nothing.

Rolling over on her hands and knees, Gwen crawled quickly to the edge of the porch. Jake lay stretched out in the shadows, the bench covering his head. The heavy wooden bench must have knocked him unconscious. She leaped to the ground, carefully moved the bench, and knelt at Jake's side. "Jake," she said urgently. "Talk to me." Running her fingers over his face, she leaned down to see if she could hear him breathing.

Steel rods clamped over her hands, squeezing her fingers tightly together. "What do you want me to talk about? That you're crazy?" Jake asked with soft menace. "Or that you're driving me crazy?" Releasing her hands, he cradled her face with his strong, work-roughened hands. "Maybe there's a better way of explaining things to you than talking."

CHAPTER FOUR

GWEN could have broken free. Could have stood up and walked away. Could have informed him she didn't kiss employees. She could have. She didn't. Instead her knees went limp, and she found herself sprawled on top of Jake. She propped her elbows on his chest. Putting space between them. "If you're thinking about kissing me, I don't think it's a good idea."

"You're right." He smoothed the hair back from her face.

"You work for me. You shouldn't kiss me."

"Maybe I shouldn't." He laughed softly. "But I sure as hell am going to." He ran a thumb along one of her cheekbones.

"I'm your boss." His body should feel hard and lumpy, uncomfortable, beneath her. Not supportive. Not comforting. Her body shouldn't melt into his. "What if I ordered you not to kiss me?"

"I'd be very disappointed." He lightly traced the outline of her mouth. "Are you going to order me not to kiss you, boss?"

Enough light penetrated the darkness to allow her to see the gleam of his teeth. She knew he smiled. "It would be silly of me to want to kiss you. I don't know you. I don't even know if you're married."

"I'm not." He slipped one hand around to her back. Warm fingers played with her spine. "Never have been."

His hand trailed down her backbone, moving over to cup her hip. Heat spread through her body. "Me neither." What an idiotic thing to say. He hadn't asked.

"I know." He toyed with a loose strand of hair which fell forward over her shoulder. "That's why I came out to apologize. While you were up putting pardner to bed, I helped Doris clean up and she told me about your brother and his wife. Doris said you were holding your brother's hand when he died, still trapped in their car. I understand now why Gordon's playing games this morning upset you."

Gwen clenched her teeth together. She wouldn't cry. "Bert must have told Doris. He talked too much."

"Doris said he worried about you." Jake hesitated. "I lost a brother, but at least I didn't see him die." Jake tried not to think about how Luther must have died. Most outlaws' lives ended violently.

"I'm sorry. His death still must have hurt."

Jake dislodged her elbows, pulling her down to rest her head on his chest. "It was a long time ago." He rubbed the palm of one hand up and down her spine. "I want to apologize for what I said this morning. If I were a woman, I might have cried, too."

Indignantly, Gwen lifted her head. "What's that supposed to mean? Only weak little women cry? Men are too strong?"

Jake pushed her head back down. "Maybe men don't know how to cry."

"Crying has nothing to do with weakness," Gwen muttered against his shirt. His chest rose and fell beneath her cheek. A woodsy soap scent clung to him. He'd showered before dinner.

Jake wrapped his other arm around her. "There are different kinds of strength. When it comes to fortitude, I've known women I'd put up against any man."

Jealousy tweaked at Gwen. "I can't help I'm only five foot five and skinny."

He chuckled. "No man's going to look at a well-formed woman like you and call her skinny."

As compliments went, it was different. Funny how the words made Gwen want to purr and stretch against him like a cat. She smiled at nothing. Comparing herself to an animal must come from dwelling in the country. "I ought to get up."

"Yup." He slid both hands down to cup her bottom. "You ought to."

"And you shouldn't be holding my—uh…"

"Behind?" he suggested softly.

She giggled. "I don't believe there's any such word."

"It's an old Texas word. And yours is an almighty soft behind."

Gwen closed her eyes and breathed deeply. Every soft, drawled word sent pleasure percolating through her body. As long as she kept talking, she wouldn't have to get up. "I suppose that's another way of saying I'm a neophyte horseback rider. That if I knew how to ride, I'd have a hard, calloused bottom."

His laugh stirred the hair atop her head. "Honey, if I thought riding would put callouses on this bohind—" he squeezed gently "—I'd never let you sit on another horse."

She thought about and discarded telling him she was the one who decided whether or not she rode. Tomorrow would be soon enough to wade into that battle again. Right now she lacked the will to fight. Maybe because his steady breathing had relaxed her to the point of mindlessness. Or maybe because she liked the feel of him beneath her. Tomorrow she'd face reality. Tonight, a gentle breeze hummed in her ears, stars twinkled from above, and one tall, dark, handsome cowboy murmured silly nothings to her. The stuff chemistry was made of. A lonesome woman and the only man on the horizon. Unless one counted Tom. Gwen swallowed a giggle.

"I felt that little laugh," Jake said lazily, threading fingers through her hair. "What's so funny?"

''You and me. We don't like each other.'' She lifted her head. ''I think you're bossy and obnoxious. You think I'm a weakling.'' She pressed her fingers against his mouth. ''Let me finish. If we passed on the street or worked in the same office, we wouldn't bother to exchange the time of day. The only reason there's this physical attraction, or whatever it is, between us is because we're the only two people of the opposite sex and a certain age on this ranch. Chemistry, proximity, call it what you will, it doesn't mean anything.''

He wrapped his hand around her fingers. ''I don't think you're a weakling. You've taken on raising a child who's not your own. You're trying to give her a good, happy life and a home.'' He pressed a kiss against the palm of her hand. ''The man who wins you will be a lucky man.'' His hand tightened around her fingers. ''I'm almost sorry I won't be around to meet him.''

The fierce, almost convulsive way he squeezed brought pain to her fingers before he released her hand. That pain waned in comparison to the pain of reality. She'd momentarily forgotten Jake Stoner wasn't a man to settle down. ''I'd better get up before someone comes outside.'' For the first time she considered the possibility of someone catching her and Jake in such embarrassing circumstances. Doris could come out on the porch. Or Tom. He was watching TV with Doris. He might decide to head over to the stone house. Either of them could come to the door to let Mack out. Rolling off Jake's warm body, Gwen struggled to her feet. ''I'm sorry you fell off the porch.''

''I'm not.'' Jake folded his arms behind his head.

''Yes, well, I'm glad you're not hurt.''

''You're leaving without kissing me. That hurts, boss lady. That hurts real bad.''

''You could have kissed me.'' Gwen froze, appalled at what she'd blurted out.

Jake chuckled. "Next time I will, boss lady. I'll kiss you until your toes tingle and jump right out of those fancy laced-up boots you wear."

His presumptuous arrogance dispelled any desire to kiss him. If any such desire had ever existed. "There won't be a next time." Wheeling about, she headed for the porch steps. Over her shoulder, she added, "You're just passing through, remember?"

"I'm not leaving before I kiss you. That's a promise." Suddenly he repeated in a loud, firm voice, "You hear that? I promised."

Gwen slammed the screen door. For good measure, she slammed shut the inside door, too.

Tom appeared in the doorway to the living room. "What's going on?"

"Nothing. A snake in the grass is all."

The old man frowned. "I better check."

"Don't bother. He's crawled back to his hole by now."

"What kind of snake?"

"The male kind," Gwen bit out. She dashed up the stairs.

"Nothing's wrong." Tom's voice carried up the staircase after her. "Jake kissed Gwen again. I tell you, Doris, he's the darnedest man for kissing women. Going to get himself in trouble one of these days."

Gwen could have yelled down that Jake Stoner was already in trouble. And that he had not kissed her. He hadn't wanted to kiss her. She didn't yell anything. Her luck, Doris and Tom would think she actually wanted Jake to kiss her.

Inside her bedroom, Gwen clutched one of the tall bedposts with both hands, tempted to bang her head against the cold brass. Bang it hard enough to knock some sense into her feeble brain. What was the matter with her? Cuddling on the ground with Jake Stoner. She

detested him. He was arrogant, bossy, obnoxious, a pain
in the neck. A man who'd always be moving on. Never
settling down. She didn't want a man with itchy feet.
Not that the kind of man she wanted someday had anything to do with Jake Stoner.

Looking up, Gwen caught sight of herself in the mirror. ''Oh, all right,'' she said crossly. ''I did want him
to kiss me. He's the only man in a million miles, and
everybody likes to be kissed once in a while. A silly kiss
doesn't mean a thing.'' It was crazy, but the face in the
mirror seemed to be laughing at her.

Jake decided honor wasn't all it was cracked up to be.
He'd wanted to rip Gwen's clothes off, shred those
damned jeans she wore. Now he knew how thirsty cattle
felt fenced off from water. Frustrated. Knowing what
was there if they could break through. Touching Gwen's
skin would be like caressing silk. Silk encasing a warm,
rounded bottom. Maybe next time he wouldn't be quite
so honorable.

He made a derisive sound. Honor. A strange word for
an outlaw to use.

He was a man with a man's needs. He'd thought about
persuading Marian to lie with him before they married,
but he'd not lusted after her the way he lusted after
Gwen. Now he wondered if, hidden deep inside him
where he could ignore it, had been the knowledge that
Marian's airs and graces masked a weak and shallow
person. She'd have sneered at the pants and man-styled
shirts Gwen wore, but all Marian's feminine ways, sway-
ing skirts, and perfumed petticoats couldn't make her
half the woman Gwen was.

Jake's body tightened at the memory of Gwen's body
molded to his length. No one could doubt Gwen had all
the necessary physical equipment in all the right places.
She might not fit Marian's definition of a lady, but she

definitely fit Jake's definition of a woman. Soft where a
woman ought to be soft.

A woman to marry and have children with. Any child
Gwen gave birth to would come out squalling lustily,
ready to take on the world. Bright, eager children. Tough
and capable. Sons and daughters a man could be proud
of.

Jake had expected to have those children with Marian.
He would have been a good father, like his pa. He'd
have shown his sons how to do things. He wouldn't have
used the whip. As his step-pa had been fond of doing.

He thought of the way Gwen rushed up to the house
to protect Crissie. He suspected Gwen would always
fight to protect those she loved. She wouldn't stand by
and watch a child of hers be horsewhipped. He had a
feeling Gwen would grab that horsewhip and use it
against the man who dared harm her child.

He'd never told Marian about his step-pa horsewhip-
ping him. Or about his ma coming to him afterward and
telling him he'd better leave. He'd known Ma meant she
was too weak to protect him, but he'd not held it against
her. Not after a while. Before he'd left, he'd even promised her, if she ever needed him, he'd be there. He'd
meant if she wanted to leave her husband. She'd asked
for help with Luther.

Marian thought he ought to ignore his mother's letter.
Told him to wait awhile and then write his mother that
he'd looked and couldn't find Luther. Marian said his
mother was far away in Texas and would never know.
Jake told Marian he would know. He couldn't refuse Ma.
Not when he'd promised.

He'd promised Gwen he wouldn't leave before he
kissed her again. He'd said it loud so Michaels would
hear, no matter where his sorry hide was.

He could have kissed Gwen tonight.

She wouldn't have objected. He hadn't kissed her because it didn't seem right. Apologizing and then stealing a kiss. Not that he would have been stealing anything. He grinned. Gwen hadn't meant to say that about him not kissing her. Light from the house had shown him the dismayed look on her face.

He should have kissed her. The next time he would.

Jake shut his eyes and remembered how good rounded, denim-covered flesh felt against his palms. His blood warmed as he recalled the soft mounds which had pressed against his chest.

Damn Michaels for sending Jake here. Tonight, when Gwen had thanked him for saving Crissie, he could have told her Crissie had never been in serious danger. He hadn't realized it at the time, but he knew it now. If Jake had been sent to save Crissie's life, once he'd done so, Michaels would have summoned him back from earth.

Which would have been fine with Jake. A dead man should be at peace. He shouldn't have stirrings in his groin.

Crissie's bed was empty. Through the heating ducts Gwen could hear her niece chattering away, with an occasional response from Doris. Gwen thanked her lucky stars for the housekeeper. She'd worried that Doris, used to keeping house for adult males, might balk at taking on a young woman and a small child, but Doris had been thrilled. A widow without children, Doris had happily taken Gwen and Crissie under her wing. Gwen didn't know how she'd manage without the other woman.

Knowing Doris had her eagle eye on Crissie, Gwen took a quick shower and dressed before going downstairs. Her hair hung damply to her shoulders.

From the kitchen came the sound of Crissie still talking. Gwen couldn't pick out Crissie's words but she smiled as her niece giggled. A smile wiped off her face by the deep-throated laugh which followed. A masculine laugh. Jake.

Gwen hesitated at the bottom of the staircase. Jake should have eaten and gone to work by now. She hadn't anticipated dealing with him until lunch. He'd saved Crissie, and Gwen was grateful, but he had to understand he couldn't continue to treat Gwen like his personal toy. She'd tell him so.

Except her mind boggled at the idea of telling Jake Stoner anything. Better to simply pretend last night never happened. Let Jake Stoner think that whatever had happened, and really, nothing had... He hadn't even kissed her. Hadn't even wanted to kiss her. Never mind that. All she had to do was greet him in a cool, distant manner, making it perfectly clear she wanted no repetition of what had happened. Not that anything had happened.

An omission she could quit harping on any second now. Kissing Jake Stoner once had been a mistake. Anyone could make a mistake. Gwen headed for the kitchen. "Good morning."

"Me and Jake is eating breakfast."

Jake looked over Crissie's head and smiled. "Sleep well?"

"Why wouldn't I?" Gwen regretted the question the minute it left her mouth. His smile changed. From casual and friendly to masculine surety. A smile which reminded her she was a woman and he was a man. Not that she needed reminding. Gwen resisted an impulse to fan herself. The August day promised to be another hot one. The kitchen was already uncomfortably warm. Gwen dragged her gaze from Jake and looked around. Doris had been baking. Pecan rolls cooled on a rack on the countertop. Relief ran over Gwen. Being hot had nothing to do with the look in a certain pair of gray eyes. It had to do with baking bread. Gwen snatched a warm roll and took a big bite. "Mmm, these are delicious." She licked a dollop of caramel frosting off her lower lip. "Absolutely yummy."

"Parades are yummy, aren't they, Jake, I mean pardner?"

"Well, pardner," Jake drawled, "yummy covers a whole lot of territory." He directed a meaningful look at Gwen's mouth.

She swallowed the bite of roll. He thought he could disconcert her at the breakfast table. He couldn't. "It looks like a beautiful day today. Is it too much to hope that I may ride outside the corral today?"

"Me and Jake is going to a parade," Crissie cried. "You can come."

"A parade?"

The kitchen timer bonged, and Jake stood up. "The Arkansas Valley Fair is taking place this week in Rocky Ford. Doris told Tom and me all about it this morning." He took an angel food cake from the oven. "It's the oldest fair in the state of Colorado, started in 1878. Today's the big parade. Doris said she and Bert never missed the fair." He gave Gwen a comically helpless look. "Do you know how to do this?"

Gwen took the cake pan from him and turned it over. Concentrating on resting the pan's three legs on the upside down mugs sitting on the countertop, she said, "I don't want to go to a fair."

"Sure you do," Jake said easily. "You and I and Doris and pardner are all going. Doris went upstairs to get ready."

"Someone has to stay here and watch the cows or something."

"Tom'll be here. Says he's too old for fairs."

"He doesn't want someone to see him who knows his son." Gwen knew Tom had arranged for a letter to be delivered to his family, but he refused to phone them.

Said his son had one of those devices on his phone which showed the phone number of the caller.

"A man doesn't want to be found, that's his business. Trust me, I know. Our business is going to a parade, right, pardner?"

"Right. Going to a parade." Crissie screwed her face up toward Jake. "Wash."

He laughed and dampened the kitchen towel. "What a mug." When he finished with Crissie's face and hands, he wiped off the table and the floor around the little girl's chair.

"Doris won't appreciate you using her nice embroidered towel to clean the floor," Gwen said, sipping her coffee.

"Doris won't mind."

Gwen refused to debate the issue. He was probably right. Doris was yet another mindless victim of gray eyes and a reckless smile. Crissie being the other victim. Not Gwen. She reached for another roll. "There will probably be drunks and pickpockets and who knows what at the parade. I moved down here to get away from all that. You and Doris go ahead and go." As if either one planned to ask for Gwen's permission.

Jake gave her a long look. "Crissie, run upstairs and get ready to go to the parade."

"She's not—" The roll shoved in her mouth cut off her speech. Gwen yanked it out. "What was that all about?"

Jake swung shut the door between the kitchen and the rest of the house. "No point in Crissie listening to us argue."

"I am not arguing. I am merely stating a fact."

Jake sat, leaning against the back of his chair. "Okay," he said in a mild voice, "let's have it. What's the real reason you're trying to spoil Crissie's fun?"

"I'm not spoiling Crissie's fun. I'm not convinced she'd enjoy a parade."

"Yeah, right. Most kids don't enjoy horses and clowns," he said sarcastically.

"She's too young."

The kitchen door swung open. Crissie peeked around the door. "Who's going to dress me?"

Jake gave her an astonished look. "You said you were almost four years old. Dress yourself."

Crissie grinned. "Okay." The door swung shut. Then opened again. Crissie popped her head through the narrow opening. "Pardner." Giggling, she disappeared. This time she didn't return.

The ghost of a smile clung to Jake's face as he turned to Gwen. "Well, Auntie Gwen? I'm waiting."

"I told you—"

"You're still mad at me, aren't you?"

She glared at him over her coffee mug. "You should have consulted me before telling Crissie she could go to the parade."

"It never..." He shook his head. "No, you're not mad about that. You're mad because I didn't kiss you last night."

"I am not. Of all the arrogant things to say."

He shrugged. "Hey, I'm annoyed about that, too, but I'm not making Crissie miss the parade."

She slammed her mug down on the table. "That has nothing to do with anything."

He raised an eyebrow in disbelief. "Doesn't it?" Before she could answer, he continued, "If it means Crissie can go to the parade, hell, even if you'd taste like pecan rolls, I don't mind kissing you right here, right now."

"I'd mind," Gwen snapped.

"You wouldn't mind." He smiled, a sexy, overwhelmingly male smile. "I'd make sure of that."

Gwen uncurled her toes. "Let's get one thing straight, Mr. Stoner. I don't know who or what you think you are, but—"

"I'm not Mr. Stoner. I'm the guy who's going to the county fair with my three favorite gals. Unless you're wearing that frosting on your face, you'd better trot upstairs and get ready to go."

Gwen opened her mouth, then slammed it shut. She had a feeling if she didn't "trot" upstairs, she'd be standing on a street corner in Rocky Ford frosted ear to ear with creamy caramel.

Crissie would love the parade. Gwen would go for Crissie.

A clown whizzed by on a motorized scooter. Crissie shrieked with glee. "Look, look! Another one."

Gwen couldn't help smiling. In her pink-checked blouse, turquoise-flowered shorts and orange stockings, wearing her shiny white dress-up shoes, with Jake's beat-up black cowboy hat on her head, Crissie could have passed for one of the clowns. "Thank you," Gwen said to Jake.

He peered around Crissie's leg. "For what? Finding this prime viewing spot?"

"For making me let Crissie come." Gwen glanced up at Crissie sitting on Jake's shoulders. The little girl squealed with excitement as two clowns on in-line skates zipped past. "You were right. I was being selfish, denying Crissie some fun for no good reason. I'm ashamed of myself. She's having a wonderful time. Thank you."

He looked at her thoughtfully. "Pretty and honest."

Gwen shrugged. "Not so honest."

Jake suddenly laughed. "As intriguing a comment as that is, I will manfully resist the temptation to poke my nose in where it doesn't belong."

"That's right. You're a man who minds his own business, aren't you?"

"When I can."

"And when you can't?"

"I do what has to be done."

"Like hauling me to a parade?"

He gave her a slow grin. "Crissie and I wanted to come to the fair. I knew Doris would be meeting up with her friends, and I was a little nervous about bringing Crissie all by my lonesome. I don't know much about little girls. Ouch."

Crissie had grabbed his hair as a clown on stilts walked over to her. Jake exchanged laughing words with the clown while a wide-eyed Crissie stared at the tall, orange-haired creature. The clown extended his hand and, after a word from Jake, Crissie cautiously placed her hand in the clown's. He solemnly shook her hand, then walked stiffly down the street.

Gwen couldn't decide which she enjoyed more. The parade or Crissie's face as she watched it. By the time the last band had marched by, the last horse pranced by, the last clown, the last automobile, the last motorcycle and the last tractor had passed, Crissie was bouncing up and down on Jake's shoulders like a yo-yo, but she still had enough energy to point out the various food vendors patroling the streets.

"Want anything?" Jake nodded toward some cotton candy.

Gwen shuddered. "I'll pass."

Jake set Crissie on the ground. "You're not eating this while you're on my shoulders." He handed Crissie a paper cone covered with a huge mass of pink spun sugar, and took back his hat. "I'd end up looking like a pink-haired clown."

Crissie danced along beside his long legs as the three of them walked back to where Gwen had parked her car.

"Jake's a clown, Jake's a clown," Crissie crowed, her mouth stuffed with cotton candy.

"You're both going to spoil your lunch."

Jake tore off a huge hunk of his candy. "I think Gwen needs a little sweetening up. What do you think, pardner?"

"Gwen likes sugar. She puts bunches and bunches on cottage cheese."

"That settles it. Open up, boss lady."

Gwen backed away. "Get that nasty stuff away from me."

"Not nasty." Crissie licked some off her nose. "It's good. Try it. You'll like it. You say that."

"I say that when I'm talking about broccoli. Not—" Her words were lost in a clump of pink fluff. The minute the cotton candy hit her mouth, the spun wisps of sugar melted against her tongue. Returning Gwen immediately to childhood. "Umm. I'd forgotten how decadent that tastes. Give me another hunk."

Jake held his cone of cotton candy beyond her reach. "Now, boss lady, I wouldn't want to spoil your lunch."

"Crissie will share, won't you?"

Crissie giggled and danced away. "Eat Jake's. Eat Jake's."

"Here." Jake's eyes gleamed with laughter as he tore off a hunk of candy. "Open wide." He shook his head. "No hands, boss lady. I like feeding you."

"Like Mack," Crissie piped up.

"Just like Mack," Jake said. "Hold out a bone and he'll follow you anywhere."

Gwen thrust her chin into the air. "On second thought, I don't want any cotton candy, and I certainly wouldn't follow you anywhere."

Jake waved the candy under her nose. "Cotton candy, cotton candy, get your cotton candy right here," he said in a low singsong voice.

Gwen's mouth watered as the sweet, enticing scent filled her nostrils. She licked her mouth once, and then, almost before she knew she was going to do it, Gwen leaned forward and closed her lips over the candy, sucking the spun sugar into her mouth. Closing her eyes, she gave herself over to the childish pleasure of feeling the strands dissolve against the roof of her mouth and searching out with her tongue every tiny undissolved crystal of sugar. Greedy for the last succulent drop, she licked Jake's forefinger and thumb.

Then realized what she was doing and froze. Melted sugar trickled toward the back of her throat. She risked a peek upward at Jake. An indecipherable something stirred at the back of his eyes. Suddenly Gwen realized her lips were still locked around his fingers. Her mouth sprang open.

Jake slowly withdrew his thumb and finger, brushing against the sensitive surface of her bottom lip.

"I'm done," Crissie announced. "I can eat yours."

Jake started, then looked down at Crissie. "Listen, pardner," he said in fake growl, "you don't take a man's horse or his cotton candy."

"I'm still hungry."

"So am I, pardner." Jake gave Gwen a long, deliberate look. "So am I."

"Well, well, well, look who's here. Uncle Bert's clever little girlfriend."

CHAPTER FIVE

THE sneering voice from behind caught Gwen off guard. It took a moment for her to switch mental gears from Jake's subtly provocative statement to the comment of a totally different nature delivered by Bert's nephew. She turned slowly, telling herself she'd explained her and Bert's friendship to Gordon as many times as she was going to explain it. "Hello, Gordon. Did you come for the parade, too?"

"I don't like the bad man." Crissie scooted over to stand behind Jake, her head peeking between his legs as she clutched his jeans with sticky hands.

Jake reached down and ran a soothing hand over her hair.

Gordon glared at them both before transferring his attention back to Gwen. "I thought you were getting rid of this gorilla. What happened? Get lonely out there in the boonies? A woman like you always needs a man around." He ran a contemptuous gaze over Jake. "A real man. You should have called me."

Jumping in before Jake reacted to the slur on his manhood, Gwen said, "How kind of you to offer to help me at the ranch, Gordon. Especially considering that you've been trying to get it away from me."

"You and me mighta got off to kind of a bad start. Maybe I was a little hasty in my judgments. I've been thinking." Gordon arranged his face in a heavy-lidded smirk. "There'd be extra-special compensation working with you."

"He's a bad, bad man," Crissie said in a little voice.

Out of the mouth of babes, Gwen thought. She

couldn't decide if the greater insult was to her principles or to her taste. How could Gordon possibly believe she'd be interested in a disgusting cretin like him? She could kick him the way he'd kicked Mack or she could pretend to misunderstand his sleazy innuendo. She chose the latter course. Innocently widening her eyes, she said, "You told Bert there wasn't enough money in the world to pay you to baby-sit cows and fix fences."

He gave her a smoldering look. "I wasn't talking about money."

Gwen feigned puzzlement. "I can't imagine what else...unless you mean, doing your taxes?"

"It's not your pencil-pushing skills I'm interested in," Gordon said through gritted teeth. "How'd you sucker in Bert if you're so damned dumb?"

"Bad man said a bad word."

"Can't you shut that kid up?"

Jake hoisted Crissie into his arms and whispered something into her ear. Crissie looked at Gordon, giggled, and buried her face in Jake's shoulder. Jake smiled serenely.

Gwen frowned at them. Gordon's presence didn't thrill her, either, but she didn't intend to start a brawl in the middle of town. Suddenly she thought of a genial CPA whose long-winded explanations drove his colleagues to dash around corners when they saw him coming. "Shutting her up is the absolutely worst thing I could do. Children have to be allowed to express themselves."

Droning on, Gwen thoroughly covered the subject of raising children, moved on to exhaust the topic of chewing tobacco, and was well into a monologue on filling out the Schedule F on Bert's tax return, the unit-livestock-price method and how to claim gasoline credit, when Gordon edged away. "Are you leaving? I'm sorry, Gordon, I have a bad habit of going on a bit about taxes.

It's a CPA curse. Nice to see you again,'' she yelled after him.

Jake chuckled.

Gwen turned on him as he stood holding Crissie easily in his arms. "I don't know why you're laughing. He insulted you as much as he insulted me."

"No, he didn't. He thinks you'd let him bed you. That's more insulting than anything he can say to me."

"Very funny. He slurred your manhood. I didn't expect you to brawl in the middle of the street, but you could have flexed some muscles or something." She'd never been an advocate of violence, but Gordon brought out the worst in her.

"Honey, a man doesn't have to prove himself every time some tinhorn runs off at the mouth."

Even if she ordinarily agreed with him, she refused to let the subject drop. Jake shouldn't have stood silently by while Gordon slimed her. "I thought out west men stood up for women." Before he could answer, she rushed ahead, "When I hired you to work for me, I expected loyalty. That means I expect you to help me. Which means any kind of help I need."

Cool gray eyes rested on her face. "That's what I thought, too, boss lady. When you need," he emphasized the last word, "help, I'll be there."

"Then why didn't you..." she began heatedly, only to sputter to a halt as his meaning reached her. "Oh. You mean I didn't need help because I handled him on my own. Thank you. I think."

"You're welcome."

Crissie tightened her grip around Jake's neck. "He's a silly man."

Gwen looked at her niece in surprise. "You think Mr. Pease is silly?"

Crissie nodded. "Jake said. Green peas. He said you'd smash him with a fork." Crissie giggled, then started singing, "Green peas. Smash, smash. Put in the garbage can. No more green peas. Smash, smash."

Gwen wanted to laugh, but parenting meant teaching the proper behavior. "It's not nice to make fun of a person's name."

"What happened to encouraging her to say whatever comes into her head?"

"It didn't come into her head. It came into yours."

Jake laughed. "You're cranky because you're hungry. Let's go get a hot dog."

"Let's go get a nice salad lunch."

"Honey, we're going to the fair. We want walking-around food, sloppy food, dribble-down-your-face food."

"We want a light, healthy meal."

"I wanna hot dog. Like Jake."

"Growing children need nutritious food."

"Wanna hot dog."

"Hot dogs make you big and strong," Jake said solemnly.

"Strong enough to smash peas?" Gwen asked sarcastically.

"Smash peas, smash peas, smash peas," Crissie sang in a cautious voice. "Hot dogs smash peas."

Gwen eyed her niece's hopeful face and Jake's challenging one. Easy for him to behave irresponsibly. The job of raising Crissie, making sure she grew up strong and healthy, didn't fall to him. His right eyebrow shifted upward. As if he read her thoughts. And questioned her conclusions. "When someone else's child is entrusted to you, you have to honor that trust."

"You honor that kind of trust with love."

Gwen blinked at Jake's flat voice. A voice which appeared to hide pain, and not the kind of voice which invited questions. She stuck with his words. "Love is the most important thing, yes, but milk and vitamins and all that other stuff counts, too.''

''Wanna hot dog,'' Crissie said in a voice which clearly indicated she was losing hope she'd get one.

''Ease up, Auntie. The world won't come to an end if for one day you laugh and play and eat hot dogs.''

''Eat hot dogs,'' Crissie echoed.

Gwen capitulated. ''Oh, all right. We'll have hot dogs. Don't blame me if you end up with mustard all over you.''

''We're also going to have laughter and play. Repeat after me, Auntie, we're at the fair and we're going to have fun. C'mon, say the words. We're not moving one step until you say the words.''

''I'm not going to say the words. That's silly.''

Jake groaned. ''Oh, I'm soooo hungry. How about you, pardner?''

''I'm soooo hungry,'' Crissie echoed dutifully, then giggled.

''You two are impossible.''

''Say it.''

''Say it, say it, say it,'' Crissie chanted.

''You can't make me.''

''Show her your hands, pardner. You want those hands hugging your nice clean blouse, Auntie? You want that filthy mug kissing you? Say it.''

Gwen backed away from them. ''I can't remember what I'm supposed to say.''

Jake's laughing eyes held hers. ''We're at the fair and we're going to have fun.''

''This is so—all right,'' she shrieked as Jake zoomed Crissie, hands outstretched, toward her. ''We're at the fair and we're going to have fun. For Crissie,'' she added.

Jake leaned over and planted a firm kiss on her mouth.

"What was that for?" Her lips tingled. "You must really like hot dogs."

"Could be." He set off down the street, his last words floating back to her. "Could be I approve of my pardner's aunt. Or it could be I like kissing you."

Hot dogs he could take or leave. Gwen, on the other hand, and Crissie... Jake hoped whatever Michaels had sent him here to do happened soon. Not that there was any danger of him falling in love with Gwen. Love was something out of dime novels. Admittedly sometimes Gwen seemed like a character out of a dime novel. Her looks. Her independence. The way she put Crissie's wants and needs before her own. Unlike Ma. He'd hurt, even hated, early on, but now he understood. Ma couldn't help it she didn't have Gwen's strength.

Hell, the woman's perfume had weakened his brain. Times had changed, but Gwen was a woman like any other woman. If she'd lived a hundred years ago, she'd have been like Ma. Needing a man to protect her from every turn and twist of fate. She'd have taken Gordon into her bed. Any man was better than no man. Sure there'd been a few women who managed without a man at their side. Tough, sturdy, pioneer stock. Or hard cases like Calamity Jane. The rest, Ma and Marian, were soft, delicate women. Like Gwen. Good for warming a man's bed.

He slanted a look at her. Laughing at something Crissie said, Gwen wiped a smear of mustard from the child's mouth. Mustard stained Gwen's own lips. He wouldn't mind licking that mustard off right here and now. He had to quit thinking about her mouth. Or her curves. Womanly curves, even if not the voluptuous curves of his Marian.

His Marian. What a laugh. Loyalty hadn't meant much to the woman who'd promised to marry him. He wondered how Gwen thought about loyalty. Not that he gave a damn about her loyalty. Unless he could use it to get her into his bed before he left.

His gaze traveled idly down her length. He wouldn't mind those long, slender legs tangling with his under the covers. Damn the covers. He'd want to see every square inch of her. He'd want her giving him that same melting smile she gave Crissie. A smile filled with love.

Irritation coursed through him. Why the hell was he whimpering about love? He wasn't some wet-behind-the-ears kid. He had one purpose for a woman. The only smiles he wanted were flirtatious ones, and the only promises he wanted, a woman could keep by raising her skirts. Those were the only kinds of promises a woman knew how to keep. Ma had promised everything would be all right when Pa died. Marian had promised to love him forever.

He no longer believed in a woman's promises.

Michaels, now. Jake believed his promises. Michaels had told him after this trip, Jake could quit coming back. He would be at peace. Jake wanted peace.

He didn't want any promises from Gwen. He didn't intend to make her any promises.

The only promise was to himself. Before he left, he'd feel those legs wrapped around him.

A momentary repugnance shook him. He was no better than Gordon. He shrugged off the feeling. Gordon thought only of himself. He'd take what he wanted. When Jake left Gwen's bed, he'd leave behind a satisfied woman. She'd have no regrets. Nor would he.

The woman's gaze passed over the three of them, moved on, then flew back to Jake. Gwen swallowed a laugh. The woman was reacting no differently than ninety per-cent of the female fair-goers. Maybe Jake's dark, good looks caught their eyes. Maybe it was his gentle way of handling Crissie. Or the sexy way he strolled along, his long legs snugly encased in worn denim. More than one woman had admired his tight behind. Totally self-possessed, his cool, don't-give-a-darn gray eyes—even shadowed by his battered black hat—seemed to throw out a challenge to every passing female. The man literally reeked of testosterone and sex appeal. He knew his worth, and every woman who came into his orbit felt a certain gravitational tug toward him.

Except Gwen, of course. She felt only amusement. Naturally she didn't mind being the envy of every woman between the ages of ten and one hundred they encountered. Having a gorgeous, sexy man at her side was another accessory, like great shoes or fabulous jewelry. The right outfit could make a woman.

The right man could make a woman, what? Happy? Smug? Forget that. Today the only emotion Jake Stoner aroused in Gwen was gratitude. She'd needed reminding that spontaneity could be healthy and good, too.

Wanting to do the very best she could for Crissie, Gwen admitted sometimes she was a tad inflexible. Monica and Dan, Crissie's parents, had taken spontaneity to its extreme. They'd loved Crissie, but on their terms. On a lark they'd decided to have a baby, and when the baby proved inconvenient, in moneyed times they'd hired a nanny; in poor times, they'd dumped her on friends and relatives or hauled her around with them. On at least one occasion they'd gone out, leaving Crissie alone. When Gwen had protested, Monica said they'd waited until the baby was asleep before leaving, as if that made it okay. Crissie had been a resilient baby, but until she'd come to live with Gwen, she'd never known any kind of schedule or consistency.

Crissie had never known a man like Jake, either. She didn't give two hoots about a handsome face or a tall, lean, muscular body or broad shoulders. The face smiled at her and the tall body and broad shoulders held her securely up above the crowds. That's what Crissie cared about.

Children and animals judged instinctively. From the beginning, Crissie and Mack trusted Jake and mistrusted Gordon. Bert's nephew almost running the child down had merely solidified Crissie's instinctive dislike.

"You wanted to ride today. Pick your horse."

Gwen looked blankly at the cardboard stub held in front of her face, then realized they stood in front of the merry-go-round. Improbable steeds of every color cavorted in a circle. Crissie pointed to a gaudy dapple gray who appeared ready to leap into space. "I'll stand and hang on to Crissie," Gwen said.

"That's what you think, boss lady." Jake hoisted Crissie onto the gray horse, then pointed to the black horse next to it. "This fellow's for you."

"Merry-go-rounds are for children. I'll watch and wave when the two of you go by."

"Hang on tight, Crissie. I have to help Gwen up."

"I'm not riding." Large hands caught her firmly around the waist, and Gwen's feet left the ground. Ignoring her protests, Jake plunked her down on the black horse. Her legs dangled down one side of the molded animal.

"Not that way, Gwen. Like me." Crissie drummed her legs on either side of her mount.

"We're at the fair and we're going to have fun," Jake said softly.

Reminding her. Resisting a childish urge to stick her tongue out at him, Gwen bent and twisted her left leg until she managed to sling it over so she straddled the horse.

"I knew it," Jake said. "He's perfect for you."

Gwen glanced down at the worn horse's head. "Why

is he perfect for me?'' she demanded suspiciously. ''He's so old even a greenhorn can ride him?''

''Greenhorn?'' Jake's mouth twitched. ''Anyone who can handle Susie, can handle this wild stallion.''

Gwen suspected the wildest stallion on the merry-go-round stood between her and Crissie, his arm resting easily on the back of Crissie's horse. The notion, entirely without basis, startled Gwen. Then music blared, and her horse jerked and began his ascent. Her leg brushed Jake's shoulders. She had to say something. ''Isn't this fun, Crissie?''

Crissie laughed, her words lost to the wind and the music.

Jake grinned up at Gwen. ''A tough cowgirl like you, maybe you ought to enter the rodeo this afternoon.''

Riding a bucking bronco couldn't make her heart thump any harder than it thumped now. Each upward and downward move of the merry-go-round horse brought Gwen's thigh into contact with Jake's rock-solid shoulder. Gwen stared straight ahead. Other parents stood beside their children. They didn't take up more than their share of the space between two horses. Jake Stoner had a devilish streak in him. He enjoyed disconcerting Gwen. ''You don't like working for a woman, do you?''

He gave her a quizzical look. ''What maggot do you have in your brain now?''

''That's why you're always harassing me. Giving me orders.'' The ride slowed to a halt, the music stopping. Gwen jumped off the horse while Jake lifted Crissie off. ''Insisting I do what you want me to do, when you want me to do it. Bullying me. I told you I didn't want to ride.'' Thinking out loud, she began to work up a head of steam. ''What I wanted didn't matter to you. You physically picked me up and forced me to ride. Maybe

I'm afraid of heights. Maybe I have something wrong with my ears so I get sick when I go around in circles.''

"Do you?"

"That's irrelevant. When I say I want to do something or I don't want something, that's my business. Not yours. Quit telling me what to do. Ouch.'' She bumped into the metal awning attached to one of the food trailers.

"You okay?"

"No thanks to you. Why didn't you tell me I was walking into that?"

"I suppose I could have told you to watch where you were going. I could have told you to duck. Thought about it.'' He shrugged. "But you ordered me to quit telling you what to do."

"You know very well that's not what I meant."

"You mean when you give orders, I'm supposed to stop and figure out whether or not you mean them before I follow them?"

"You are deliberately twisting my meaning."

"Did you know your eyes kind of sparkle when you get annoyed? Like sunlight bouncing off a wet frog. Stay here and hold Gwen's hand.'' Putting Crissie on the ground, Jake walked away.

Gwen stared after him, not sure whether to laugh or throw her purse at him.

"Jake's nice. I like him."

Gwen looked down at her niece. "Crissie Mary Ashton, you have rocks in your head."

Crissie shook her head back and forth. "Don't hear rocks.'' She looked up past Gwen. "Do you got rocks in your head?"

Jake rejoined them. "Did Gwen say I do?"

"Me.'' Crissie shook her head again. "Don't hear them.'' Looking up, her eyes widened. "I wanna go up. Way up."

Gwen absentmindedly gave Crissie's hand to Jake. "My eyes make you think of a wet frog?"

"Only when you're annoyed. When you're pondering, I think of a little backwater place I know in Texas along the Guadalupe River in the shade of big ol' overhanging cypress trees where the water moves slow and sluggish like thick, green molasses." Jake's soft drawl caressed the words.

Gwen mentally shook off their mesmerizing effect. "If wet frogs, sluggish water and green molasses are your idea of compliments, I hope you never get around to insulting me."

His gaze held hers. "Now, honey, you wouldn't by any chance be bad-mouthing my favorite spot on the river, would you?"

She watched in fascination as currents swirled around in gray eyes. Something warm flickered and disappeared in the back of his eyes. Replaced by cool amusement which brought Gwen to her senses. "Don't call me honey."

"Yes, ma'am, boss lady." The amusement deepened.

Welcoming the tug on her leg, Gwen looked down.

Crissie's eager face beamed up at her. "I wanna ride." Crissie squeezed Gwen's leg. "Ride around."

"Around what?" Gwen belatedly realized Jake had guided them into a line for a ride. She looked up. Way up. "We're not riding the Ferris wheel. Crissie is too little."

"Don't worry. She's safe with me. She'll love it."

The line they stood in advanced toward the ride. "I'm not getting on the Ferris wheel," Gwen hissed at Jake.

"You'd trust Crissie to ride alone with me?" Jake asked in surprise.

"No. Yes. That's not the point." Only one couple stood between them and the head of the line.

"What is the point?"

Gwen bit her lip. She didn't want to say it in front of Crissie.

After a second, Jake said gently, "Trust me, honey. Nothing will happen to you as long as you're with me. I'll keep you safe."

They were next. The attendant stopped a seat, pushed back the safety bar and waited for them. Jake walked up to the ride, set Crissie down in the middle of the seat and turning, held out his hand to Gwen.

"Hurry up," Crissie said impatiently, kicking her feet.

Gwen wanted to cut and run. She couldn't. Not when it seemed the entire population of Colorado stood in line waiting to get on the ride. They'd all see her. And know what a coward she was. Gwen moved slowly toward the seat. Crissie's kicking made it swing. Gwen thought about the seat swinging on top of the arc and her stomach churned. Barely noticing Jake's look of approval, she gingerly climbed in beside Crissie and sat. The seat rocked as Jake added his weight. The attendant snapped the safety bar into place, tested it, then pushed the seat into the air. Gwen's stomach headed for her toes. Grabbing the bar, she squeezed her eyes tightly shut.

Sitting between Gwen and Jake, Crissie let out a shriek. "We're swinging. Swinging really high."

Some things Gwen really didn't want to know. As they rose, her hands gripped the safety bar so hard she knew her knuckles must be white. The Ferris wheel stopped. Stopping was worse than moving. The seat swayed and Gwen swallowed a moan. A hand firmly squeezed her left hand, then slid past. A steel arm pressed against her below her breasts. Gwen opened her eyes a slit. Placing his right hand between her hands, Jake bent his elbow so that his arm fenced Gwen and Crissie against the back of the seat. Gwen cautiously opened her eyes a smidgen more. They had stopped at the highest point on the ride. Her eyelids snapped back down.

"Sit very still," Jake said to Crissie. "Don't move a foot, or a leg, or a hand. You're a little bird sitting up in a very tall tree. You don't want the other birds to know you're here."

"Why not?" Crissie asked.

"It's a bird game."

"What kind of bird game?"

"Um, you're looking for worms. The bird who stays the stillest gets the most worms."

"Worms. Yuk!"

Gwen almost smiled at Crissie's revulsion. It would serve Jake right if Crissie lost her lunch all over him. She considered saying so, but with a lurch the ride started again. They swooped toward the ground. Gwen's hat caught the wind and sailed away. She didn't even bother to look. The wheel went around again and again and again. Gwen squeezed her eyelids tighter.

"You make it worse when you close your eyes."

"I'll bet you've never been, uh, whatever, in your life."

"Bet me twenty kisses that I haven't?"

Gwen's eyes popped open. "Certainly not."

"Ten kisses?"

"Dream on."

"Five kisses."

"No."

"How about one long, wet, sloppy, very enthusiastic kiss?"

Gwen swallowed hard. "I don't..." She cleared her throat. "There's no way to bet on something like that. You could tell me anything so you'd win."

"You think I'd lie to you?"

"I don't know." She hesitated. "Would you?"

His face closed up. "Only if I had to."

"Had to," she repeated thoughtfully. "And what would force you to lie to me? Winning a bet? Getting your own way?"

Jake's eyes danced with laughter. "I don't have to lie to get my own way."

"I was quiet and didn't move," Crissie chorused. "I get worms. I don't wanna eat 'em."

Jake laughed. "How about popcorn instead?" He held out his hand to Gwen. "Don't tell me you want to ride again?"

Gwen shook her head and looked around. The wheel had stopped at the bottom and the attendant waited impatiently for them to get off. Gwen jumped up and rushed down the ramp, avoiding the eyes of those in line. At the bottom, she grabbed Crissie's hand and stomped off down the wide row between the rides.

Jake caught easily up with them. "Popcorn's this way."

Gwen skidded to a halt. Jamming her fists against her hips, she glared at him. "That was a low-down dirty trick, Jake Stoner."

He had her hat. Knocking it against his thigh to remove the dust, he plunked it down on her head. "What was? Taking your mind off the ride or not winning the bet so you could give me a kiss?"

CHAPTER SIX

GWEN straightened her hat. "I didn't make any stupid bet." Holding Crissie's hand, she moved on through the fairgrounds. "You know very well you couldn't have come up with one stupid thing you've ever been afraid of. And no," she said as he opened his mouth, "I don't want to bet."

"Afraid you'll lose?" Jake strolled along at her side.

Crissie yanked on Gwen's hand. "I want popcorn."

"You are a bottomless pit," Gwen said before turning to Jake. "All right. Name one thing you've ever been afraid of in your entire life."

"Green eyes."

"I knew you couldn't come up with anything."

"There's popcorn." Crissie jumped up and down between them. "Popcorn. Popcorn."

Jake bought three boxes of popcorn and handed them out. They walked slowly toward the animal barns.

"Horsewhips," he said conversationally. "When my step-father was drunk."

Startled, Gwen turned to stare at him, a handful of popcorn halfway to her mouth. "What?"

"Even riding hell-for-leather around a herd of stampeding wild steers in the middle of a night storm didn't scare me as much as that damned whip did when I was growing up."

In Gwen's world, men didn't whip children. "I thought cows didn't stampede anymore." She fastened onto the part of the conversation she could deal with. "Bert said Texas cows were the ones who did that. On cattle drives."

"Bert was right."

"But you just said..."

Jake winked at her. "You ought to know a man'll say anything for a kiss."

"It didn't work, because I didn't believe you. Not for a single second." Not about the stampede. The whipping she wasn't so sure about. Something about Jake's eyes. She repressed a shudder and welcomed Crissie's squeal.

"Look!" The little girl ran toward a circular pen where a few small goats milled around.

Before Gwen could react, Jake caught up with Crissie, capturing her mid-dash. "Slow down, pardner. You don't want to scare the animals." He handed Gwen their popcorn boxes, and led Crissie to the enclosure's gate.

Gwen stood outside the pen watching as Jake, down on one knee, sheltered Crissie with one arm while he coaxed a baby goat over to them. Gwen couldn't hear their conversation, but Crissie gingerly held out one hand. The small kid sniffed at her fingers, then licked. The popcorn, Gwen thought, as Crissie giggled. Another goat crowded up to them, and then a third. When a fourth shoved his way in, Jake stood up, balancing Crissie on his hip. Both were laughing. One of the goats rose up on his hind legs, and Crissie's excited voice rose above the fair hubbub. She thought the goat was dancing.

When the two rejoined Gwen, Crissie bubbled with excitement. "Did you see, Gwen? Did you see? They liked me. I wanna goat."

Gwen laughed. "You want everything."

"Gonna see rabbits now," Crissie said importantly. "Jake said."

They toured the rabbits, the chickens, the ducks, the sheep, and the llamas, Crissie alternating between holding her nose and making animal sounds which she in-

sisted the animals understood. By the time they reached
the cow barn, the little girl noticeably lagged.

"I think it's time we headed for home," Gwen said.

"No. More fair."

Catching Gwen's eye, Jake ruefully shook her head.
"She's got more energy than I do. I need a nap. And I
know just the place to take one."

Jake stretched out on the blanket, his hands folded beneath his head. Beside him, Crissie's small chest rose
and fell as she slept. She was a cute little kid. He kind
of liked the way she trailed around after him, looking
up at him as if he were some kind of god. Even if it
was only because she had no father. All kids needed a
pa. No one knew that better than he did.

He'd wanted sons to carry on his name. Carry on with
the ranch. Take over the cattle empire he'd been building. His mouth twisted derisively. A man never knew
what would destroy his dreams.

Glancing down at Crissie, he noticed Gwen had
missed a smear of mustard on the child's mouth. He
hadn't thought about having girls, but that would have
been all right, too. Girls to dangle on his knee and care
for him in his old age.

Except he didn't have to worry about growing old.
His life had ended at age thirty-one.

Crossing his booted feet, Jake tipped his hat over his
face. He had a feeling it'd be a while before he saw
Gwen again. Doris had told him about the historical museum housed in the old Carnegie library building. She'd
said Gwen wanted to visit the museum, but she'd never
had the time or opportunity. Since Doris had arranged
with Jake to meet here so she could ride back to the
ranch with them, Jake had guided Gwen and Crissie to
the large parklike lawn and sent Gwen inside while he
and Crissie rested in the shade. Gwen had halfheartedly

argued she couldn't dump Crissie on him, but she'd been moving toward the museum even as she protested.

Jake didn't understand why history interested Gwen so much. He'd lived it and preferred modern times. Gwen always smelled of some exotic soap. He wondered how she'd have liked washing up in a basin or heating water to fill a metal bathtub. He grinned. Or how she'd like outhouses in the middle of a winter night. She thought nothing of hopping in the car and driving into Rocky Ford this morning. Used to be, covering twelve to fifteen miles a day, it would have taken most of a week to move cattle that far.

Gwen openly envied people with what she called "roots." People who stayed in one place. Back when he was alive, most people Jake knew were on the move. Searching for something or running from something. His ma hadn't wanted to leave her kinfolk in Tennessee, but Pa wanted his own land. Gwen was like Pa. Taking on something they knew nothing about, armed only with their dreams.

There'd been a time when Jake had dreams. Dreams which included a big house, like some of those around Gruene in Texas. He'd started to build that house, and then Ma's letter had come. His ma didn't come out and say it, but reading between the lines, Jake knew his step-father had taken to whipping Luther, too. Jake had been lucky, hiring on with honorable men. Luther had fallen in with bad company and become an owl-hoot, as many called the outlaws in Jake's day.

Marian had been appalled when Jake decided the only way to find Luther was to look for him on the owl-hoot trail. Jake wondered what Gwen would think if she knew he'd been on the owl-hoot. He suspected she'd think if that's what he had to do to find his brother, then that's what he had to do.

Footsteps moved across the grass. Beneath the brim

of his hat, Jake cracked open one eye. Doris's shoes came into view, then Doris as she lowered herself to the edge of the blanket and opened a book. He'd speak to her in a minute.

A poke in his side wakened Jake. From long habit, he lay still, feigning sleep. Blue-jean clad knees rested inches from him. His hat hid the owner of the jeans from his view. A hand pressed tightly over his mouth. Disoriented from sleep, Jake couldn't remember where he was. Was he alone? Why was he sleeping during daylight hours? Covertly he slid his hand down along his side. His gun was gone. Something prodded him again. Not a gun. A finger. Without further thought, Jake flipped his body over on the intruder, snatching the hand over his mouth, and at the same instant, grabbing the hand poking him in the side.

"Oomph. Get off, you idiot."

The low voice hissing in Jake's ear immediately swept away the lingering remnants of sleep. Gwen lay pinned to the ground beneath him. A state of affairs he didn't exactly find displeasing. The look on Gwen's face suggested she didn't share his opinion. He levered himself off her. "Sorry. You took me by surprise."

Gwen made a frantic shushing motion, then pressed a finger against her lips and pointed to the blanket with her other hand. Jake followed her pointing finger to where Crissie slept on, unperturbed by the fracas. Doris winked at him. He turned back to Gwen. She rose to her feet and brushed off her jeans. Motioning him to follow her, she stalked off without a backward glance.

Jake strolled along behind Gwen admiring the scenery. A stem of grass clung to the back of her jeans. He contemplated slowly brushing it off. Fitting his hand to the curve of her backside. A glance at the tautness of her spine and he reluctantly reconsidered the notion. Amazing how much a man could read in the thrust of a woman's shoulder blades and the flounce of her hips. Gwen was one riled lady.

If she wasn't so anxious to show him her fantastic discovery, she'd fire him on the spot. And that would bring the number of times she'd fired him to how many? Really effective all those other firings had been, hadn't they? Her jeans fit too snugly. She could feel Jake's eyeballs burning a hole in them. She whipped around. "Quit staring at my behind."

Jake chuckled. "Honey, you are purely a pleasure to know."

"And what does that mean?"

"Means what it means."

"Thank you very much for that illuminating explanation."

"You're really on the prod, aren't you? I apologized once for jumping you. I don't intend to do it again."

"Don't use that self-righteous tone of voice to me. If you will recall, Mr. Stoner, I'm the one sinned against. You attacked me."

"You shouldn't sneak up on a sleeping man."

"Excuse me. Next time I'll hire a brass band." She stomped up the wide steps to the museum. Inside the building, she pointed to a donation jar. "Put some money in there."

"Yes, Ma'am."

He didn't have to grin at the woman caretaker like that. As if he knew Gwen was being irrational and unreasonable, and he was humoring her. Grabbing Jake's arm, Gwen pulled him toward the other end of the large room. "I didn't tell you to come in here so you could make eyes at every single female who crosses your path."

He came to a dead stop, slid his hands in his back

pockets and gazed coolly at her. "Pull in your horns, honey."

No matter how soft the tone of voice, it wasn't a request.

Gwen puffed up indignantly. "Don't you tell me to pull in my horns. You work for me, mister. I'm the boss."

His eyes narrowed.

Gwen swallowed. When he looked at her like that, he reminded her of the picture. "Never mind that now. Look." Turning, she pointed to the scrap of newsprint on the top of a low cabinet. A pane of glass covered the paper, protecting it. "Why didn't you tell me about your famous ancestor?" Brushing Jake to one side, Gwen leaned over the newspaper and read the headline out loud. "'Outlaw Killed In Bank Holdup.' I thought at first he must be your great-great-grandfather, but apparently he had no children. How was he related to you?"

Jake stared down at the 1886 newspaper. "He's no ancestor of mine."

"He must be. You have his name. Jakob Stoner. And he looks exactly like you. Oddly enough, he was the same age you are. I can't believe you never heard of him."

"There was nothing to hear."

"Don't be so dense." Gwen practically danced in exasperation. "This man, this outlaw, has to be an ancestor of yours. You could be clones of each other." Gwen scanned the article again. "According to this, Jacob Stoner was supposed to marry a Marian Olson, but they broke up when he became an outlaw." She glanced up at Jake. "Do you suppose she rejected him, and he became an outlaw because of a broken heart?"

"How would I know?" he asked in a flat voice.

His attitude annoyed her. "Don't be such a wet blanket. Jakob Stoner must be your great-great-uncle or something. "It's romantic having a part of the Wild West in your background."

"That's romantic? Being related to some scourge of the West?"

"He was hardly that. In fact, he'd been a leading citizen. He'd worked for Charles Goodnight, you know, of the Goodnight-Loving Trail?"

"I've heard of it."

"He was a trail boss for Goodnight. How funny. An ancestor who was in the same kind of business as you."

"I'm not sure 'funny' is the right word," he said dryly.

"Working with cattle must run in your family. What did your father do?"

"He was a builder."

"Oh," Gwen said, disappointed. She quickly rallied. "How about your grandfather?"

"Builder. All builders. As far back as I know, which covers before they came over from Germany. The name used to be Steiner until the first Steiner to land in America changed it. Steiner means stonecutter." He grinned at her. "Aren't you going to say cutting stones is romantic?"

Intent on proving her point, she ignored the gibe. "What did your brother do?"

He hesitated. "He was involved with banking."

Gwen saw the hesitation and knew instant remorse at callously reminding Jake of his deceased brother. After a short, awkward silence, she returned to the article. "This Jakob Stoner was apparently a real up-and-comer. After he quit driving cattle, he was a lawman. Deputy, sheriff, federal marshal in places like Creede and Deadwood and Abiline. He was even a Texas ranger for a while. The article said he came from Texas. Like you."

"I never said I came from Texas."

"No, you didn't say, but I assumed." She glanced sideways at Jake. "Where did you come from?"

"Lots of places," he said curtly, studying the newspaper, a frown on his face.

Discovering an outlaw on his family tree obviously displeased him. Perhaps her theory would cheer him up. "I think the woman drove him to a life of crime."

"Only a weak man would be influenced that way by a woman."

"Losing someone you deeply love could change a person. It could," she insisted as Jake raised a skeptical brow. "Couldn't a woman drive you to desperation?"

"Want to try it and find out?" he drawled.

"No." Gwen looked down at the newspaper article again. For a moment there, the look in Jake's eye, or maybe residual shivers from riding the Ferris wheel... She almost said yes, she'd like to drive him to desperation. Forcing herself to breathe deeply, she stared at the words until they quit blurring. "It's strange someone in your family never told you about him. He wasn't all that bad."

"The man was shot while robbing a bank."

"Maybe there were extenuating circumstances."

"We're back to the woman, I take it."

"The reporter certainly seemed to think she was a raving beauty. He said, just a second, where was it? Oh, here it is, and I quote, 'As Miss Olson, with her own cherry red lips'—who else's lips would she use?—'described how the desperado had turned his back on her, the tears of sorrow glistening in the soft blue eyes of one of the loveliest and noblest blossoms of western womanhood melted this hardened reporter's heart.' I think I'm going to be sick."

"Then let's go."

"No, wait, there's more. He describes her as having 'rose petal pink cheeks,' 'alabaster skin' and, my personal favorite, 'a halo of shining chestnut curls, as silky as the finest embroidery floss.''' Gwen rolled her eyes. "He's not describing her, he's making love to her. He goes on, blah, blah, blah... 'The very picture of a broken heart, the delicate young lady burst into a despairing flood of tears at the notion of her beau deserting her for the owl-hoot trail.' Barf." Gwen looked at Jake. "Do you know what an owl-hoot trail is?"

"Means he became an outlaw."

"Probably to get away from her." Gwen sniffed in disgust. "Talk about self-centered. If she was supposed to be so crazy about him, why isn't she grieving?" She tapped the article. "Ms. Noble Blossom isn't upset he's dead. She's mad he walked out on her."

"You can't have it both ways," Jake said in amusement. "A second ago you claimed he'd become a bank robber because she kicked him out."

"In those days when a man asked you to marry him, you had to play games. He asked her to marry him and she turned him down. The dummy, oops, excuse me, I forgot he was your whatever uncle, whether you think so or not. Anyway this Jakob Stoner obviously didn't play the game and come back and ask her again. Maybe there wasn't any foreign legion or whatever for him to run off to, so he joined up with the Hole in the Wall Gang or some gang like that."

Jake gave her a sharp look. "What do you know about the Hole in the Wall Gang?"

"I go to the movies. Everybody knows about Butch Cassidy and what's his name. Anyway, Jakob runs off, and she's seriously annoyed he didn't ask her again to marry him."

"Supposing you're right, and I'm not saying you are, why did he become an outlaw? Why not return to his ranch and forget her?"

"That's easy. Revenge. He didn't just become an outlaw. He robbed banks. Get it? Marian Olson's dad was a banker.''

''According to the paper, that's not the bank he robbed.''

''Of course not. Jakob still loved her. He wouldn't do anything to hurt her.''

Jake stared at her in fascination. ''That is the damnedest bunch of claptrap I—''

''Look at the facts,'' Gwen said impatiently. ''He'd started from nothing and was building himself a future. The people the reporter interviewed had nothing but praise for Jakob. Some had even tried to get him into politics. He'd carved his ranch out of the hills, used his own sweat and muscle to put up buildings. Jakob Stoner intended to be someone. And Marian Olson intended to be Mrs. Jakob Stoner.''

''I didn't read that in the article.''

''It sticks out all over in what she says and doesn't say. She's plain annoyed. Not only did he run off, when he dies, he dies a hero. A hero who rejected her.''

''I think you need to rein in that imagination of yours.''

''Don't be as dumb as that reporter,'' Gwen said tartly. ''Marian's 'despairing flood of tears' was nothing more than her throwing a good old-fashioned temper tantrum.''

''I meant Jakob Stoner didn't die a hero.''

''Did you read this article at all?''

''I read it. Without all the fancy embellishments you're giving it. The man was shot robbing a bank.''

''No, he wasn't. He'd already robbed the bank. He could have gotten safely away, but he turned back to save a little boy who ran out into the street. Guns were blasting and horses going crazy, and Jakob leaped off his horse, grabbed the child and carried him to safety. Some storekeeper shot Jakob in the back as he returned to his horse. Jakob didn't even have his gun out. He was as good as murdered.''

''He was robbing the bank. Better to be shot in the back than be the honored guest at a necktie party.''

''Necktie party. You mean they would have hanged him?''

''In those days people didn't take kindly to having their life savings forcibly removed from the bank.''

''I don't care what you say. I agree with the minister. Maybe Jakob Stoner did take a wrong fork in the road, but at heart, he was a good man. The minister ought to know. It was his son Jakob saved.''

''All he needed was the love of a good woman,'' Jake said sarcastically.

''Go ahead and make fun of me, but if that Marian had had one lick of sense, she'd have grabbed Jakob the first time he went down on his knee. Not only must he have been one of the best-looking, sexiest cowboys in Colorado, he was clearly destined to be rich and powerful. Ms. Noble Blossom blew it.''

''You think he was good-looking and sexy?'' Jake asked in a casual voice.

Gwen opened her mouth, than clamped it shut. Words echoed in her head. Words she'd said earlier. Words pointing out how much Jake looked exactly like the man who must have been his ancestor.

Lightning flashed over the distant mesa. The scent of approaching rain drifted through the open window on the night air. Mack padded into Gwen's bedroom, his toenails clicking on the wooden floor, silent when he crossed the small area rugs. ''Can't you sleep, either?''

The large dog paused to look at Gwen, his eyes reflecting the light she left on in the hallway for Crissie.

Sitting up, Gwen punched her pillow. ''At least your problem isn't a big mouth.''

Mack moved over to the open window, and rose up, his huge paws resting on the sill. He stared out into the night.

"What do you think, fella? Is it going to rain? Does the coming storm bother you?" She remembered hearing a coyote serenading the moon earlier. "Or did you hear a pretty little lady coyote singing love songs? What makes you think she's singing them to you?"

The dog dropped down from the sill and moved over to the side of Gwen's bed.

"Why are you looking at me like that? Did I insult you by suggesting she sang to a coyote lover instead of you? You're as conceited as that arrogant you-know-who out in the bunkhouse. And I don't mean Tom. Tom would have ignored my little gaffe, but no, not Jake. He wasn't even embarrassed at being called good-looking and sexy. Not that I was calling him that."

The large dog whined.

"I was not. I simply made an observation about a historical figure. It was no different than commenting on George Washington's wooden false teeth or Abraham Lincoln's height. Jake didn't have to pounce on my words the way your coyote friend pounces on unwary rabbits."

Mack returned to his perch on the windowsill.

Gwen continued to air her grievance. "He swaggered out of the museum like he was the world's greatest gift to women. Just because he somewhat resembles a long-lost relative he'd never even heard of."

Mack trotted back over to Gwen and woofed softly.

"Mack, I let you out before I came to bed. You can't have to go out again."

The dog woofed again, impatiently this time.

"You're as bossy as he is." Gwen threw back her lightweight covers. "All right. I'll let you out, but hurry up about it." Not bothering to throw on a robe or look for her slippers, she trailed Mack down the stairs. In the darkened front entryway, she sensed the silent dog at her side as she unlocked the door. "I expect you to do your business and then come right back in here. You hear me?"

Mack shot out the door the second Gwen opened it. The yard lights illuminated the dog's bristling ruff and laid-back ears as he leaped from the porch and streaked into the night.

"Mack, just get back here," Gwen hissed, reluctant to yell and wake up the household. She didn't need anyone to tell her what an idiot she was for turning Mack loose shortly after she'd heard a coyote. Hindsight was always twenty-twenty. He'd be okay.

She rooted around on the floor of the coat closet. One of these days she'd have to decide what to do with Bert's clothes. Finally unearthing an old pair of his boots and a misshapen sweater, Gwen threw them on and headed off in the direction Mack had gone. Not that she was worried about him. No coyote would mess with a dog of Mack's size. When she got far enough from the house, she'd yell. He'd come when she called him. Mack wasn't so dumb he didn't know who'd saved him from the big dog pound in the sky. She hoped.

Lightning forked to the south. The storm was moving closer. It would serve Mack right if she left him out here to get soaking wet. Pulling the sweater tighter around her, Gwen tramped across the yard, her feet slipping halfway out of the large, old boots with each step. Under her breath she called Mack every cursed name she could think of.

A man's faint shout reached her ears. The voice came from the horse pasture. What in the world would Jake or Tom be doing out there at this hour of the night? Mack barked and the horses snorted. The answer suddenly came to Gwen as she heard the thudding of horses' hooves. Jake and Tom were gathering the horses to put them in the barn. She'd read horses were terrified of fire. Lightning must affect them the same way. The men might need help. Stepping out of the circle of illumination shed by the ranch lights, Gwen paused a moment to get her night vision. Then she followed the road along the line of fence toward Mack's barking.

Halfway to the horse pasture, the skies opened up, pouring icy water on Gwen's head. The rain did little to dampen Mack's barking. If anything, the dog sounded more frantic. Suddenly a car's engine sprang to life, the unexpected sound shocking Gwen. She stopped, peering through the driving rain. Car headlights shot out of the darkness, pinning her in their beams. She shielded her eyes with her hand, blinded by the glare. "Jake? Is that you?"

The sound of spinning tires answered her. Whoever it was, was in a hurry. Gwen squinted into the light. The vehicle revved its engine louder, broke loose from its muddy snare, backed around to face the other direction and tore off down the road. Gwen had a vague impression of a long, dark shape before red taillights disappeared over a rise.

The horses milled noisily about in the pasture, but Mack no longer barked. "Mack! Mack, come here!" Listening intently, Gwen heard only the rain and the horses. "Mack, where are you?" She headed toward the area where the vehicle had been parked. "Mack?" He must have chased the car. Gwen cupped her hands around her mouth and yelled the dog's name as loud as she could. Mack didn't answer. She couldn't abandon him out here in the rain. He could be hurt.

Walking cautiously down the side of the road, Gwen called Mack's name. With each new flash of lightning, she stopped and looked around. No wet, bedraggled dog appeared. Gwen shivered. Only her feet were dry. If she hadn't walked so far from the house, she'd go back and wake Jake. She could imagine his reaction if she showed up at the bunkhouse door looking like the drowned rat she now resembled. At least she was spared that.

A piercing whistle came from behind her. Gwen's heart stopped, then pounded in triple time. She spun around and stepped off the road into the side ditch. Her body fell like a game of Crack the Whip. Her head being the tail end of the whip. She landed facedown, half in and half out of the barrow pit, stunned, her nose digging a little trench in the muddy bank. A loud splashing noise rushing toward her barely registered. She turned her face out of the mud, but refused to open her eyes.

"Are you all right?"

She knew that voice. She didn't lift her head. "Did you whistle?"

"For Mack. I heard you calling him. Here he comes now. Are you going to spend the night there?"

"Yes."

"In case you haven't noticed, it's raining."

"What difference would that make to me? I'm in my own private swimming pool. Even if the water is a little on the muddy side. And not exactly warm. But then, I didn't stop to think about that when you came up behind me making banshee sounds and scaring the living daylights out of me."

"Is that why you fell?"

"Fell? No, Mr. Stoner, I didn't fall. I always come outdoors in the middle of a rainstorm and leap headfirst into a muddy barrow pit. Don't you?"

"No, but then, I'm not real fond of snakes."

CHAPTER SEVEN

"SNAKES!" With a screech, Gwen struggled to stand. Halfway to her feet, she discovered her oversize boots had filled with water and were now firmly embedded in the muddy bank. She yanked her legs to dislodge the boots and promptly lost her balance. Teetering wildly, Gwen windmilled her arms in a frantic effort to keep from falling back into the water. One flailing arm smacked Jake as he squatted beside the ditch, and he reached out to grab her. At that precise moment, Mack trotted over and poked his nose in Jake's back. Jake pitched headlong into the ditch.

Knocking Gwen down again. At least this time she didn't fall face-first.

Jake rolled off her and stood. "You okay?" He extended his hand.

"Go away." Gwen sat up in the muddy water and swiped at her face with the mud-soaked sweater. "If there are any snakes around here, I want to make sure I'm the one they bite." She yanked a boot out of the mud, turned it upside down to drain the water, then tossed it up on the road. "Dying from snake venom would at least put me out of my misery." She grabbed the second boot as Jake vaulted from the ditch. Not bothering to drain the second boot, Gwen threw it at Jake as hard as she could. She missed him. Ignoring his outstretched hand, she clawed her way out of the barrow pit. Pushing wet stringy hair out of her eyes, she looked for the boots. She found one by stubbing her big toe on it. Muttering under her breath, she rammed her foot into it. The other boot had disappeared. "Where's my boot?"

"Mack's got it."

"Mack, bring me the boot."

The dog put the boot down, barked happily, then picked it up and backed away as Gwen hopped on one foot toward him.

"He wants to play."

Gwen heard the quiver of amusement in Jake's voice. "I'm glad you're having such a good time. I'm wet, I'm freezing, and I probably broke my nose. And I want my boot."

"Come, Mack." Jake snapped his fingers, and Mack trotted over to him and dropped the boot at Jake's feet. Jake picked it up and held it out.

Gwen ripped it from his hand, shoved her foot inside, and marched toward the house, wiping dog slobber off on her sweater.

"Want to tell me why you're taking an evening stroll in the rain?" Jake easily kept pace with her.

"I'm giving myself a facial, what do you think?" The rain would at least wash the worst of the mud off.

"I think you have a better reason than that."

"I'm not paying you to think." The furious words had barely left her tongue when she remembered and grabbed Jake's arm. "Didn't you see him?"

"Who? Mack? He's right here."

"No. I don't know who. Mack wanted out and he raced straight out here to the horses. I went chasing after him to haul him back in the house and I heard a man's voice. I thought you and Tom were moving the horses because of the coming storm, so I came to help you, and then this car started up. Mack must have scared off whoever it was. The driver shone his headlights right on me, so he had to see me, but he hit the gas and took off, Mack apparently in hot pursuit. Then it started raining, and you came sneaking up behind me making me fall into the ditch, and Jake, the horses!" Gwen wheeled about and trotted awkwardly in the big boots back toward the pasture. "What if he hurt the horses? We have to check the horses."

"I'll check. You go back to the house and get dry and warm." Jake leaped easily across the ditch, then turned at the splashing sound behind him. "Damn it, Gwen, do you ever do what you're told?" Grabbing her outstretched hand, he pulled her up to his side of the ditch.

"They're my horses." He could make all the disgusted sounds he wanted to make, but they were.

"Watch out for the barbed wire."

"Ouch. You could have mentioned that earlier."

"You could have gone back to the house."

"I couldn't now even if I wanted to. I thought you checked the fence along here. I'm caught on a broken wire."

"Not broken," Jake said grimly. "Someone cut the top two strands of the fence.

She struggled to break free. Jake made no move to come to her aid. Finally she said in an exasperated voice, "Would you please help me?"

"No. At least I'll know where you are while I'm checking the horses. Come on, Mack."

"Don't you dare walk off and leave me stuck here," she shouted at Jake's back. Man and dog vanished into the dark. "I swear, if I knew how to use that old buffalo gun, I'd shoot you, Jake Stoner." A person would think he owned this ranch the way he ignored her orders. She'd get loose and then she'd show him exactly who was the boss around here.

Getting loose was no small chore. The severed wires, curling back on themselves, had not only thoroughly snared the back of her sweater, a few of the barbs had worked through the sweater's ragged, loose weave to catch in the T-shirt beneath. The fabric being wet didn't help, but at least the rain seemed to be easing. If she couldn't remove the sweater from the wire, Gwen decided the next best thing was to remove herself from the sweater.

A loud noise came out of the dark. The sound of something being crunched under large feet. Gwen froze. "Mack?" Clouds blocked out the moon and the stars, and she strained to see. A large dark shape detached itself from the inky black night and moved toward her, snuffling as it moved. One of the horses.

Gwen remained stock still, her mind racing. What if the horse couldn't see her and ran right into her? Or equally bad, got tangled up in the cut wires. If she called Jake she might frighten the horse into bolting into the fence. A scenario which boded ill for both her and the horse. Maybe if she spoke softly. Words refused to leave her closed throat.

Hot breath blew against the back of her head, and the horse gave a low nicker. Slowly turning her head, Gwen saw a splash of white down the horse's nose. "Hello, Vegas," she cautiously crooned. "Are you okay? Big, bad man didn't hurt you, did he?"

"The horses all seem to be fine." Jake had returned. "Everyone accounted for. You and Mack evidently chased off whoever it was before he did any real mischief. If the fence hadn't been cut, I'd figure it was kids stopping to pet the horses. I moved the other horses into the next pasture. You can ride Vegas back to the house."

"I'm not going to ride Vegas back to the house."

"You need a hot shower."

"I do not need a hot shower. I am sick and tired of you telling me what to do. Go away." She swallowed a startled cry as Mack poked her bare thigh with his cold nose. "And take this stupid mutt and this stupid horse with you."

"You're the boss." Jake walked away, whistling at the dog and horse to follow him.

Gwen stared at the three dark shapes in stunned disbelief. Jake Stoner was actually going to abandon her. Furiously she struggled to get out of the snared sweater without jabbing herself with the barbed wire. She was cold, wet, filthy, firmly attached to a fence, surrounded by who knew what kind of wild animals... Darn wool sweater. It didn't even have the decency to rip. A coyote yipped in the distance. Did coyotes attack people? Gwen redoubled her efforts.

A rustling sounded near her feet. She turned to stone. Snakes. Jake had mentioned snakes. Surely no self-respecting snake would be out on a night like this. They'd be curled up nice and cozy in their dens. They wouldn't come out until it stopped raining. Her heart almost stopped when she realized the rain had stopped. Forcing herself to breathe slowly, she told her wavering courage the high leather boots would protect her.

"If you're waiting for a rainbow, they're kind of hard to see in the dark."

She practically leaped out of her boots. Worried about snakes, she hadn't heard Jake return. She'd be darned if she'd admit either her fear or her predicament. "I love being outside after a rain. The air always smells so clean. Washed by Mother Nature," she said airily. Not for a million dollars would she ask him again to rescue her. "There's almost something spiritual about it."

"You want me to leave you alone to commune with nature?"

"No," she said quickly. Quelling her moment of panic, she added, "I'm through."

"Then let's go back to the house."

Gwen let him take about three steps before she folded. "Darn you. Get over here and free me."

"I thought you ordered me to go away and leave you alone."

"Since when have you started paying the least bit of attention to anything I tell you?"

Jake chuckled. Stepping easily over the bottom strands of wire, he walked around to face Gwen. "This is the damnedest job I've ever had."

"Nobody ever bothered the horses where you worked before?"

"I've dealt with plenty of horse thieves and cattle rustlers." He made no move to help her. "I've never dealt with a woman as cussed stubborn as you." He added in amusement, "Or as wet and dirty."

The last remark wasn't worthy of comment. "Why is it when women have opinions and aren't total wimps, men think they're stubborn or bossy or demanding?"

"Why is it women always think all men are the same? I certainly don't think you're like any woman I've ever met."

"Why do I doubt that's a compliment?" When he merely laughed instead of insisting it was, she asked tartly, "Are you going to free me or stand there and admire the scenery?"

"If you're giving me a choice, I'll admire the scenery."

"I wasn't," she snapped. "Besides it's too dark to see anything."

"I wouldn't say that. I have a good view of you."

"Fine, and when you're through laughing at my muddy face, do you suppose you could set me free?"

"I wasn't looking at your face." He paused. "Interesting outfit you wear when you're gallivanting around the countryside."

The evening's commotion had driven out of Gwen's head any thought of what she wore. The man's large white T-shirt barely reached the middle of her thighs. "I was in bed. I suppose you sleep fully dressed."

"Actually, since you asked, I wear less than you do."

She was glad darkness hid the blush heating her skin. "I wasn't asking." Hopefully, the darkness also hid the way the wet knit fabric clung to her skin.

Jake laughed and moved to her side, his hands busy with the coils of wire. "I don't know how you managed to entangle yourself this way."

High above, the clouds parted, and the half-moon bathed the landscape with soft light. And gleamed on the bare shoulder inches from Gwen. Unable to stop herself from looking down, she breathed a silent sigh of relief when she saw Jake wore jeans and boots. He'd neglected to fasten the top button of his jeans. What held them up? She couldn't drag her fascinated gaze away. Jake turned and bent over, swearing at the wire. His jeans were in no danger of falling down. The rain had plastered the wet denim to his tight bottom.

Jake maneuvered his hands under Gwen's sweater, moving up her back to carefully work her T-shirt off the barbs. His hands warmed her through the cold, wet shirt. She wondered how work-roughened fingers would feel against bare skin.

"You okay?"

"What? Yes, why?"

"You started breathing harder. You're just about free. Don't panic now."

"I'm not panicking." Her voice sounded funny.

Jake evidently thought so, too. "You sound hoarse. Damn. I should have made you go back to the house the minute I got out here."

"You couldn't make me."

"I could have made you." He pulled on the wire. "There. Your shirt's loose. Leave the sweater. I'll get it tomorrow." He guided her arms out of the sleeves. "Climb over the fence." Standing on the bottom wires until they almost touched the ground, he practically lifted her over. Vegas ambled over at Jake's whistle.

"Where's Mack?" Gwen asked.

"He went back to the house. He's no dummy."

"Meaning I am?"

Jake tossed her on Vegas's back and vaulted easily on behind her. "How long would I have a job if I called my boss a dummy?" Pulling her back against his heated body, he turned the horse toward the house.

"Since when has that been a consideration to you? You don't go away when I do fire you." Cold and tired now the excitement had ended, she'd like nothing better than to curl into him until he'd warmed every inch of her to the same degree his body warmed her back. "Have you always been so darned determined to do things your way?"

"I've been accused of it in the past." He tightened the arm encircling her under her breasts. "I wonder what would have happened if we'd both have lived a hundred years ago."

"There would have been two Jake Stoners running around the country. You and your outlaw ancestor." Gwen bounced with every step Vegas took. Each bounce created friction between her and Jakes's bodies. She tried to concentrate on his words. Conversation would distract her from the strange sensations muddling through her body. "You probably would have fought over Marian Whosit, Ms. Noble Blossom." Gwen disliked the woman more with each passing reference. "There'd have been two of you robbing stagecoaches to forget a broken heart."

"Jakob Stoner never robbed a stagecoach." Jake shifted, his jean-clad legs brushing her bare skin.

Gwen's fingers curled in Vegas's mane. "How do you know?"

"The newspaper would have mentioned it. What makes you think I'd be like him?"

She started to say their similar physical appearance, but instead blurted out, "Your arrogance."

Jake rested a hand on her hipbone. "Would you care to explain that?"

She'd explain. If she could think about something besides wanting to rub against him. She focused on his question. "You're always telling me what to do. You think you know best. A person only has to look at his picture to know he was the same." She considered that, then said slowly, "Which means, whatever he did, he must have believed he had good reason. That it was the best thing to do at the time."

"What happened to him being driven by a broken heart?"

Gwen turned to look up at Jake. "I don't think you'd let a woman get close enough to you to break your heart."

"I thought we were talking about the other Jakob Stoner."

The dark hid his expression from her. "I'm not sure there's much difference. I've never thought much about reincarnation, but maybe he wasn't finished down here, so he came back as his great-great-great-whatever nephew."

"And who are you supposed to be? The fair Marian?" he asked, his voice heavy with sarcasm.

Gwen shook her head. "I wouldn't have let you— him—go." She felt his unseen eyes boring into her.

Jake halted Vegas. Shifting Gwen so her head rested against his shoulder, he ran a finger along her cheek. "You think a half-dressed, muddy-faced woman could stop me?"

Her breath caught. "If I were her, I would have tried to stop Jakob."

He slid his fingers down to wrap around her chin. "What makes you think Marian didn't try?"

"She didn't love you. I mean, him."

"You don't know that." He tipped her chin up.

"Yes, I do." She swallowed hard as he trailed fingers down her throat. "She would have been bereft, inconsolable, locked in her room. Not dressed in fancy clothes, giving interviews."

"The article said she cried." He threaded fingers into Gwen's damp hair and traced the whorls of her outer ear.

"Crocodile tears. To show off her blue eyes." Her lips parted as he lowered his head.

"Jakob Stoner was an idiot," he muttered. "He should have found himself a woman with green eyes. A woman with kiss-me lips."

The words puffed warmly against her face and then his mouth covered hers. Gwen forgot about wet shirts, damp boots, a filthy face and scraggly hair. Nothing existed for her except the heat of Jake's mouth. Expecting the type of gentle kiss he'd given her before, she was stunned, then aroused, by the unexpected fierce hunger of this kiss. He kissed her as if the kiss had to last him for an eternity.

Vegas stamped an impatient foot, and Gwen clutched at Jake's thighs for balance. Not that she needed it. His arms held her securely.

His large hands moved to spread over her breasts, warming them until they swelled to fit his palms, her nipples greedily demanding more of him. He curled his thumbs around the hard tips. "When I came here, I wasn't expecting you."

"You're kind of a surprise to me, too, cowboy." She shivered as his thumbs brushed her nipples in a caressing gesture. Vegas stamped his foot harder. "I'm cold. I'd better go in." Gwen didn't want to leave his arms.

"Yes." Jake slowly removed his hands from her breasts. "It's been a long day."

Vegas needed little urging to cover the remaining distance. Gwen clutched at Vegas's mane as they bounced along. Exquisite awareness of Jake filled every fiber of her being. The unexpectedness of his kiss filled her with uncertainty. How did he feel about her? What thoughts were going through his mind?

He silently guided the horse through the barn corral to the darkened ranch house. Easily dismounting, Jake reached up to help Gwen down. "It has been a long day," he repeated his earlier remark, "but a good day."

"Yes." His hands warmed her waist. "Thank you for insisting I take Crissie to the fair. She had a wonderful time."

"So did I. Can I ask you one thing?"

She thought of Tom's answer. "You may ask. Mebbe I'll answer and mebbe I won't."

He laughed softly, and dropped a light, appreciative kiss on the tip of her nose. "Why are you so afraid of Ferris wheels?"

It was about the last question she expected, and it took a second to gather her thoughts, to decide whether to tell him the truth. He brushed the back of his hand across her cheek, settling the question. She was starting to care for this man. Which meant she had to be honest with him, no matter how humiliating the truth was.

"When I was twelve, four of us were on one. A girl I'd just met and two boys. The boys were showing off, and started swinging the seat. The other girl thought it was funny, but I was terrified and started crying. When we got to the bottom, the man running the wheel made us get off. He was furious and gave the boys a long sermon about safety. They all blamed me because I'd cried, said he wouldn't have cared if I hadn't been such a baby. My dad had just been transferred there, so I was a new kid. We were there for two years and I hated it the whole time. The kids never stopped teasing me about being such a coward.''

''I may not know much about you, boss lady, but I'm pretty sure about one thing. You're no coward.''

''Thank you.'' She hesitated. ''Why did you ask?''

''I wanted to know.'' He tugged playfully on a strand of hair. ''Go in and take a hot bath, put on a warm nightgown and get into bed.'' Turning her around, he nudged her toward the house with a light swat on the rear end. ''Now, go.''

Tossing his wet towel across the bedroom chair, Jake climbed between the sheets. Nobody and nothing, short of a box of dynamite, was going to rouse him out of this bed until the sun came up. Nothing at all. Nobody. His mouth twisted in wry acknowledgment of the lie. One somebody could. One whistle from the big house and he'd race up there faster than Vegas ever trotted over to his call.

Just his luck to learn too late that green eyes and a generous mouth packed a more dangerous punch than a trainload of nitroglycerin. Damn it all to hell, he should be beyond being affected by a woman like Gwen. A fact certain overactive parts of his body couldn't seem to remember. He hoped Gwen hadn't noticed.

Not, he thought with satisfaction, that some of her parts hadn't responded with equal fervor to their kiss. He could still feel her tight nipples digging into his palms. That skimpy shirt she wore had outlined her every luscious curve. Hell's fire, he'd wanted to strip it off her and kiss every inch of bare naked cold skin. He'd have warmed her up fast. One look at her had warmed him up fast enough.

He shifted uncomfortably in the bed. Thoughts like these wouldn't help him sleep. He forcibly turned his mind to the newspaper article Gwen had found in the museum. The article amused him in an odd sort of way. Not many men had the dubious privilege of reading about their own deaths.

Gwen hadn't noticed the two things in the article of most significance to Jake. Most important, no mention was made of Luther. The paper said the other four bandits had escaped. The posse had lost them. So Luther had lived. That time. Not many bank robbers enjoyed long lives. A fact Jake had tried to drum into his younger brother's head time and time again. Luther was young enough he still thought he was invincible. Jake had told him no man was invincible against lead. He wondered if Luther believed him after the bank robbery had gone wrong.

Six bullets had brought Jake down. He'd liked the way Gwen's eyes had sparkled with indignation, but she'd been wrong calling it murder. Just as he'd been wrong in how he'd gone about trying to get Luther to quit the business. Instead of trying to talk sense into the kid, he should have thrown a rope on him, tied him to a horse, and ridden hell-bent for leather out of there. Instead he'd jawed on and on until he'd gotten as tired of listening to his words as Luther had.

Jake had wanted to believe the others had listened when he'd pointed out shooting people they robbed wasn't smart. Dead men had relatives. A man could rob a bank in Kansas and go on a spending spree in Montana, knowing most lawmen wouldn't bother you if you stayed clean in their town. A man with revenge-minded relatives on his trail was lucky if he could sit at a campfire long enough to boil a pot of coffee. The gang's leader had backed Jake in this, but Jake wasn't naive enough to believe the outlaws wouldn't shoot if they didn't think it necessary. And there was nothing to keep the victims from shooting back. Knowing this, Jake had ridden with the bunch with the idea of protecting

Luther until he could get his brother to leave the owl-hoot trail.

Robbing the bank had been the fourth time he'd ridden with the gang. He thought about Marian talking to the reporter. She would have insisted on seeing his body. To make sure the dead man was him and not Luther. Maybe she'd have felt a twinge of remorse when she counted the six bullet holes.

Jake frowned. He'd been careless earlier. Running out without his shirt when he'd heard Gwen yelling for Mack. You'd think he'd remember, but he didn't feel the wounds. The first second, there'd been unbelievable, searing pain, then nothing. The bullets weren't in him. The undertaker had probably taken them as souvenirs of the time he laid out the great bank robber, Jakob Stoner. But Gwen would question the scars.

Gwen. His thoughts always returned to her. He'd wanted her so badly tonight, he'd hurt. That had never been true with Marian. Abstaining until marriage had been no hardship. Not sleeping with Gwen made a lot of things hard.

Had Michaels thought about what a woman like Gwen could do to him? Michaels probably figured Jake had no needs. Michaels had erred. Maybe this whole business was as mystifying to Michaels as it was to Jake. Michaels had never answered Jake as to why Jake hadn't been sent straight to perdition. Maybe Michaels knew; maybe he didn't. After today, Jake knew. He'd read it in the newspaper. The minister said he and his wife were praying for Jake's soul.

The trail boss upstairs had heard their prayers. He'd answered them in his own way. He'd given Jake another chance. Ten chances to be exact. Ten chances to help people. Ten chances to redeem himself.

There had been one terrible moment tonight when he'd hesitated to go outside. When he'd wondered if

Gwen's need of his particular help awaited him. He never knew what he was sent to do. He only knew that when he'd done it, he left. He wasn't ready to leave Gwen. For an instant, he'd selfishly considered not going to her aid. If he didn't go out, if he pretended he didn't hear Mack, if he didn't help her, if she managed on her own...

He wished he could remember his other nine visits back. Had his help made a life or death difference? That's what he didn't know. And not knowing, he couldn't risk Gwen.

Whatever the reason he'd been sent to help Gwen, he knew one thing with certainty. Once he'd done his deed, Michaels would take him away. In saving Gwen, he'd lose her. Forever.

Jake stared sightlessly at the ceiling. Gwen had called Jakob Stoner a hero. He wasn't a hero. He was a man who'd done what he'd had to do. He couldn't let that little kid get hurt. Any more than Gwen could refuse to care for her brother's kid.

He was no hero. Just a man who wanted a woman. Not any woman. Gwen.

Gwen couldn't remember the last time she'd awakened with a smile on her face. But then she'd never before gone to sleep thinking about Jake Stoner's kisses. After he'd told her to go take a shower, she didn't think his next words were meant for her ears, but she'd heard them over the clip-clopping of Vegas's feet as Jake had led the horse down to the corral.

"Go," Jake had said, "before I take you into my bed to warm you up."

One of these days Jake Stoner was going to say something like that and Gwen would march right into his arms and tell him to do it. One of these days. When they got to know each other a little better. When she worked up the nerve. Rolling over in bed, she kept her eyes shut and imagined the scene played out a million different agreeable ways.

The ringing phone interrupted her pleasant reverie. Reaching out a bare arm, still smiling, Gwen picked up the receiver. "Good morning to you," she sang out.

A short pause ensued. "Gwen?"

"Yes, it's Gwen, and this is a lovely day and how are you, Prudence?"

"It's cloudy and overcast."

"Good," Gwen said. "I have developed a positive affection for rain."

"Do you feel okay?"

"I feel super. Why?"

"You sound a little funny."

"I suppose I'm coming down with a cold. We had some trouble here last night and I got a little wet." Gwen wanted to laugh at the understatement.

"Trouble." Prudence sighed heavily. "I was afraid of that. That's why I called. Was Jake Stoner involved in any way in your trouble?"

Gwen thought about Jake untangling her from the severed barbed wire. "You could say that."

"Damn. I should have dug deeper, questioned how he showed up out of the blue like that. I'm sorry, Gwen. This is all my fault."

Gwen's smile faded. She sat up in bed, and chilled, pulled the covers up over her lap. "What are you talking about? Who showed up? Do you mean Jake?"

CHAPTER EIGHT

"I WENT looking because Gordon was making all kinds of noises about taking you to court over inheriting the ranch from Bert. He threatened to say you brought undue influence on Bert and a bunch of nonsense like that. No one who knew Bert would believe it, but to substantiate your claim if Gordon actually filed a suit against you, I researched the old records. They were interesting little pieces of old history, and I got carried away. Even dug out some old forgotten records buried in the basement of the courthouse. That's where I found it. Or actually, didn't find it."

"Find what?" Apprehension crawled up Gwen's spine.

There was a long pause before Prudence said carefully, "The title to Bert's ranch isn't quite as clear as I'd like it to be."

Gwen crumpled the sheet in her fist. "What does that mean?"

"The land was claimed and filed on by one Jakob Stoner back in 1881."

"Jakob Stoner owned this ranch?" Gwen asked in astonishment.

"Yes, and when he died—"

"He was shot."

"How do you know that?"

"Never mind. Go on."

"Jakob Stoner left the land to his brother, Luther."

"Jakob had a brother?"

"Yes. Luther, along with his infant daughter, died in 1889 in a carriage accident. I found a copy of the death

117

certificate. Then the records show a Gordon Winthrop leaving the ranch to his sons in 1921.''

"Gordon? As in Gordon Pease? Are you saying Gordon Pease really does have some kind of claim on the ranch?''

"Not Gordon. What's missing is any record of the ownership of the ranch transferring from the Stoners to the Winthrops. There's a number of ways Winthrop could have legally acquired the land. Relinquishment, for example. But if he didn't get it legally, then a case might be made, if Luther Stoner left any relatives, they should have inherited the ranch. And any descendants of those relatives could make a claim against the property.''

"The ranch never belonged to Bert's family? It belongs to descendants of Jakob Stoner?''

"I'm sure it belonged to the Winthrops. There's just no proof,'' Prudence said unhappily. "Stoner descendants could claim the Winthrops acquired the land illegally and claim it belongs to them. Over the years the Winthrops have made improvements, buildings, windmills, et cetera, so that would be in your favor, but the whole mess could be tied up in court for years. My guess is the Stoners somehow or other found out about the ranch and are snooping around to see if there's anything in it for them. Unless they have some pretty concrete proof, a court battle would be as costly for them as for you. I think the Stoners saw a single woman with a child and no knowledge of ranching and thought they could intimidate you. Get you to settle with them out of court.''

"You keep saying the Stoners.'' Gwen dug her fingers into the mattress. "You mean Jake Stoner, don't you?''

"I've asked around. I can't find anyone who's ever met him or even heard of him before. Maybe the name is a coincidence, and there's nothing to be concerned about.''

Gwen thought about the picture in the old newspaper article. "It's no coincidence," she said flatly. "I have to think about this. I'll talk to you later." She hung up the phone, her hand shaking.

Jake Stoner planned to steal her ranch. To take away her home. Gwen stretched the sheet between her fists. If he wanted to steal the ranch, why come here and work for her? Why waste time kissing Gwen? He must know those kisses wouldn't influence her if they faced each other across lawyers' tables or in court. What did he hope to do or learn here? Gwen knew nothing of the early origins of the ranch.

The answer came with heart-stabbing clarity. Jake hadn't found the missing papers, either. He'd kissed Gwen with one purpose in mind. To romance himself into her bed and into her house. He must believe the papers were hidden somewhere in the main house. Sleeping with Gwen would give him an excuse to be in the house all hours of the day and night. He could search for the missing papers.

Gwen went down to breakfast determined to have it out with Jake. She'd debated not letting him know his secret was out, but there didn't seem to be any advantage to that. She needed a ranch hand, but she didn't need a disloyal one. An ugly thought halted her on the staircase. Was Jake somehow involved in cutting the fence last night? Had he been kissing her to allow his confederate to escape? Or to come back and complete his mischief? That thought sent her racing into the kitchen.

"About time, lazybones," Jake drawled as Gwen burst through the door. "Tom and I got up with the chickens. I fixed that fence, and Tom doubled-checked the horses. He says they're fine."

She'd ask Tom herself. "Where is Tom?"

"Outside with Crissie. They're teaching Mack a new trick."

"Oh." Gwen poured a mug of coffee, silently castigating herself for becoming so discombobulated she hadn't even noticed her niece wasn't at the table. Another reason to deal with the situation now. To deal with Jake now.

Jake refilled his coffee mug. "Soon as you eat, I thought we'd take a ride. Check out the other fences and the cattle. You might want to think about moving the cows and calves away from the main road."

She fixed herself a bowl of cereal. "Why?"

"In case our midnight visitor comes back with other ideas."

"I don't see the point of him letting the cows loose."

Jake shrugged. "Could be lots of reasons. Scatter them to cause us bother. Steal them."

"Cattle rustlers in this day and age?" Removing her toast from the toaster, she carried it with a knife, butter and jam to the table. Did he really think to distract her with something so ludicrous? "I doubt it."

"You think crime stopped with the twentieth century?"

"Crime, no. Cattle rustling, yes."

"You're wrong. The only difference between one hundred years ago and today is that cattle rustlers have changed how they operate. Tom says they drive up to the pasture, cut the fence, load a cow or two in the back of a pickup and sell it to a friendly butcher. Easy money for a rustler."

"Then why would he cut the fence where the horses are?"

"Maybe he thought there were cows there. Maybe he was after the horses. Could sell them to someone who's not too picky about where the horses came from. Or sell them for slaughter. That's probably the safest. Nothing left to trace."

Gwen stared speechlessly at him. Vegas and Susie

killed for a few dollars. Surely Jake wouldn't be a part of anything so wicked. She forced herself to probe. "I didn't realize what kind of outlaws we still have around. Shades of your ancestor, Jakob Stoner."

"Jakob never rustled beeves, and he wasn't a horse thief."

"Speaking of Jakob, what was the name of his brother?"

"Luther."

"Luther," Gwen repeated slowly. "How do you know that?" Jake slanted her a quick look, then picked up his spoon and stirred his coffee. Gwen knew he drank it black.

"I could have read it in that newspaper article at the museum," he finally said.

"No, you couldn't have. There was no mention made of Jakob Stoner having any relatives. No," she said as he opened his mouth, "I didn't miss it. I read that article so many times I practically have it memorized. That's not how you found out Jakob had a brother named Luther."

Jake sipped his coffee, studying her over his mug. "Maybe Luther isn't his name. Maybe the name just popped out."

"Slipped out, don't you mean? It would be very strange that the correct name of Jakob's brother would hit you out of the blue. Luther isn't exactly the commonest of names."

"It was pretty common then."

"Something else you learned in your research?"

"Research?"

"I should have caught on when you knew so much about the area. Too much for a man no one from around here has ever heard of."

Jake set his coffee mug firmly on the table. "Why

don't you quit pussyfooting around and tell me what's going on?''

"Funny you should say that. I was going to suggest the same thing to you.'' When he didn't answer right away, Gwen said impatiently, "Don't bother trying to invent some stupid fairy-tale story. I know exactly why you're here."

"You know?"

"Prudence called this morning and told me all about it. Your secret's out, Mr. Stoner. You have one hour to be off the premises or I'm calling the sheriff to escort you off."

"If this is about that kiss last night, I apologize if I—"

"It's not about the kiss and you know it. It's about why you're here."

A deep frown creased his forehead. "Prudence is your lawyer, right? How would she know why I'm here?"

"Stop it, Jake," Gwen said, weary of his cat and mouse game. "She told me about the missing papers. I can forgive a lot of things, but not lying. If you'd have come to me and told me, we might have been able to work something out. Now I'm going to fight you. Bert left this ranch to me, because it meant something to him, and he knew it would mean something to me. Bert knew Gordon would get rid of it as soon as he could. Lawrence Hingle is dying of cancer. Doris is staying on for now, but she told Bert she didn't want her future tied to the place."

Gwen pushed away her food. "Bert left me more than some land and cows and horses. He left me his ancestral home, his heritage. The Winthrop legacy. It's more than inheriting some land. Bert left me a home. I don't care if your outlaw relative did live here. Jakob Stoner died robbing a bank. Surely that forfeits any rights he had. Bert said Gordon Winthrop fought for this land. He worked hard to hand the ranch down to his sons and their sons. Bert handed it down to me and I'm not going to let you take it away from me.''

''Gordon Winthrop? You never told me Bert's last name was Winthrop. He was descended from Gordon Winthrop?''

''His grandson.''

''I'll be double-dog damned,'' Jake said softly. ''So Gordon Winthrop got his filthy hands on the place after all.''

Gwen bristled. ''I don't know what you think you know about Gordon Winthrop, but Bert told me his grandfather was a fine and honorable man. The kind of man who helped build our country.''

''Built it on the backs of other men. When Winthrop came into this part of the country most of the land was taken. He bought up a few small places whose owners sold out after their herds were stampeded or their barns burned. He wanted my, that is, Jakob Stoner's land for the water.''

''You said 'my.' My what? My ancestor's land? Is that what you were going to say? You knew all along about Jakob Stoner. You knew he was an outlaw and you knew how he died. You knew Luther—''

''Whoa. Slow down. How do you know about Luther? What do you know about him?''

''What difference does that make? The point it is, he—''

''Tell me about Luther.''

Taken aback by Jake's implacable tone of voice, Gwen stared across the table at him. No one looking at the hard face, the stony jaw, the granite eyes would ever doubt this man descended from outlaws. Her stare grew puzzled. Meanness didn't knot arm muscles or make shoulders so tense they were almost painful to look at. Something about Jakob Stoner's brother Luther affected

Jake in a strange and powerful way. Gwen's eyes widened. ''Was Luther your great-great-grandfather or something?''

Jake looked at her as if she'd lost her mind. ''Where'd you get a crazy idea like that?''

''He seems to matter so much to you.'' She paused. ''No, that's not it,'' she said slowly. ''What you want to know is where he was killed, isn't it? You think I know where the accident was. Why does it matter? Do you think he had the papers with him? You don't even know where he and his baby were going.''

Jake opened and closed his mouth several times before he managed to say in a strangled voice, ''Luther had a baby?''

''Of course he had a family. Where do you think you came from? His little girl was killed, but there must have been more than one child.'' Another thought struck her. ''Unless there was a third brother. Was there?''

''Luther had a wife and child,'' Jake said softly, almost reverently. ''I'll be double-dog damned.'' He shook his head in pleased disbelief. ''He must have married Marian.''

''I expect you know very well whom he married. You know all—'' Gwen choked on her coffee. ''Ms. Noble Blossom? He married her? You're related to her?''

''No, I'm not—'' He stopped abruptly. ''I'll be double-dog damned.''

''You already said that,'' Gwen said tartly.

He gave her a weird look. ''You know, honey, I believe, in a way, I might be related to Marian Olson. I'll be—''

''Yes, I know. Double-dog damned. You already said that. What is so funny?''

''Me. And Marian,'' he choked out between guffaws.

Gwen tapped the handle of her spoon on the table, waiting impatiently for Jake to control his hilarity. When his laughter finally subsided to a few chuckles, she said, "I'm glad you find this so funny, but I am not the least bit amused, Mr. Stoner. And don't call me honey. I don't permit people who are trying to steal my ranch out from under me to call me anything other this Ms. Ashton."

"Whoa, back up there, honey. I think I missed something in the conversation. You're accusing me of trying to steal your ranch?"

Tears pricked the back of Gwen's eyelids. She'd liked Jake Stoner. Liked his kisses. Was starting to like the slow, intimate way he said "honey." As if she were someone special to him. She'd even been foolish enough to dream about a future with him. A dream which Prudence's phone call had shot to smithereens. Anger had thus far sustained her. Now sorrow and grief for the loss of what might have been overwhelmed her. Her shoulders slumped. "Don't do this, Jake. Don't play games."

"Well now, honey," he drawled, "seems to me, if any games are being played, you're the one dealing the cards. I sent you off to bed last night thinking I'd been dealt a royal flush. This morning I appear to be looking at a busted hand. Why don't you lay it out plain and tell me what has you madder than a wet hen?"

"I told you. I know why you're here."

"I thought I was here to help you, but if you know something different, maybe you ought to tell me what it is."

His cautious tone of voice damned him. He wasn't about to say anything she could use against him in court. Jake Stoner had been playing her for a sucker from the moment he'd waylaid her on the street in Trinidad. She'd trusted him, and he'd returned that trust with betrayal. "I don't care if those darned papers are missing. Gordon Winthrop acquired this ranch through totally legal means, and no one will convince me otherwise. Not one cow, not one inch of ground, not one blade of grass belongs to you.''

"To me?''

He overdid it with the fake astonishment. Keeping her voice level, Gwen said, ''I don't care how many buried wills or titles or whatever you find in my house, it's my house and my ranch and you and the rest of your Stoner relatives can't have it.''

Crissie's laughing voice floated through the open kitchen window as the little girl called to Mack. Mack yelped in happy excitement. They'd moved from the front porch to the back of the house. Gwen heard Doris's voice from the direction of the garden. Doris liked to weed before the day grew too hot.

Trailing around after Tom, helping Doris, playing with Mack, Crissie had blossomed on the ranch, her little legs strengthened, her face lightly tanned. She was a different child from the little girl who'd cried for her mama and daddy every night last year. And then cried again when left at the day-care center. The pediatrician said Crissie was too young to understand what her parents' deaths meant, and too young to understand Gwen had to go to work but would always return for her after work. All Crissie knew was her parents had abandoned her and she could never be sure Gwen wouldn't do the same. For Crissie, the ranch not only meant a fun place to play, it meant security. Gwen would never allow anyone to take that security away from Crissie.

No one. Not even Jake. No matter how magically he kissed.

Jake sat motionless across the table; his entire body might have been carved from stone. His closed face hid his thoughts, but Gwen sensed his intense concentration as he sorted through the implications of what she'd said. He needn't bother. There was no way he could convince her he hadn't been serving her a dirty, rotten, underhanded trick from the moment he'd engineered a meeting with her.

He roused, stood, and walked over to the coffeepot to refill his mug. His back to her, he asked slowly, "You think I'm here to take the ranch away from you?"

"Doesn't matter. You can't."

"This is a complication I hadn't anticipated."

"Thank you so much," Gwen said sarcastically. "It's nice to know you assumed I'd be stupid and easy to manipulate."

Jake turned and leaned against the cabinet, sipping his coffee. "You're not stupid," he said absently. His eyes focused on a point somewhere behind her.

Dismissing her. Saying she wasn't stupid in a tone of voice which clearly conveyed his total lack of interest in her as a person. He was a liar, a manipulator, a swindler, and a hypocrite. Pretending he enjoyed kissing her. Kissing her stupid. And she was stupid. A co-worker in Denver had once said Gwen had a brain like a computer. If so, her computer had severely malfunctioned. She'd liked Jake's kisses. Liked him. Thought he liked her.

And all the while he'd been kissing her, he'd been plotting to steal the ranch from her. He was worse than pond scum. Worse than head lice. If the old well wasn't boarded up, she'd push him down it. Not once had he denied coming here to steal the ranch. Not that she'd believe any worthless denials. "Now that your filthy little secret's out, I see no point in feeding you and housing you and giving you access to whatever it is you're hunting for. I want you to leave. Any further communication between us will be through lawyers."

"I'm going to check the rest of the fence this morning. Make sure our late-night visitors didn't cut any other wires. We can talk about this later."

Gwen put her hands in her lap. Safely away from her knife and the temptation to use it to carve her words into his forehead. "There's nothing to talk about. You have one hour to pack. If you need a ride, Doris or Tom can take you to town in the pickup." Her voice barely wobbled. Not that Jake Stoner would notice if she fell down on the floor and pounded the speckled linoleum with her fists in a grade-A tantrum. His entire concern was himself, the ranch, and how he could manipulate her past this turn of events. He couldn't.

Jake started to say something, obviously changed his mind and headed for the back door, in passing lifting his wide-brimmed hat from the rack hanging by the door. His back to Gwen, he paused in the open doorway to carefully position his hat. "I don't think it works like this," he said in a vague, preoccupied voice. The door closed behind him.

Gwen wanted to scream after him that it worked exactly like this, but she couldn't. She was incapable of any speech. She could only try to swallow over the huge, painful lump in her throat.

Granada casually ambled over at Jake's whistle. Jake blew lightly into the large bay gelding's nostrils. "Taking your own sweet time so I won't think I'm the boss, aren't you?" The horse nickered a soft greeting, and Jake patted the bay affectionately. He'd miss the horse when he left.

Not that he was considering packing. He'd leave when Michaels wanted him to leave. Gwen wouldn't like it, but Jake had no more choice in the matter than she did. Not much he could do about her accusations, either. She'd never believe the truth.

Funny how she and this Bert took to each other. Not that Gwen wasn't an attractive woman. Jake had thought about her in his bed from the moment he'd seen her, but Winthrop didn't appear to be that kind of man.

Unlike Winthrop's grandfather. Jake had seen the way

Gordon Winthrop lusted after Marian. Winthrop hadn't dared approach her while she was Jake's woman. Jake's mouth twisted. He'd been so busy worrying about riff-raff like Winthrop, he'd missed what was going on under his nose. He'd brought Luther back to the ranch for a spell, and by the time Jake realized Marian never smiled at him like she smiled at Luther, it was too late. Luther, with his good looks and easy, devil-may-care charm, had already bedded Marian before returning to his outlaw friends without a backward look. Marian had come crying to Jake.

If the irony of the situation escaped her, it hadn't escaped Jake. He now realized what he'd thought was love was merely his way of trying to climb above his humble beginnings. He'd fought hard to be the kind of man other men didn't brush aside. Or use a whip on. He'd wanted a big place with a fancy house and a fancy wife. Marian with her airs and graces, her banker father and her expensive silk dresses had seemed perfect.

Jake smoothed the saddle blanket on Granada's back, then turned to lift his saddle from the top rail of the corral. Activity across the way caught his eye. Leaning on the rail, a half smile on his face, he watched as Gwen came out the back door and called for Crissie. Gwen with her intelligent eyes and expressive face wouldn't know a fancy air if it bit her on her nicely rounded, denim-clad bottom. Crissie ran from the garden, her plump, outstretched arms waving madly. Mack loped along behind the child.

Gwen's crystal-clear laughter easily reached Jake at the corral as she practically danced from the house to meet her niece halfway. Gwen didn't need silk dresses and French perfumes to be a woman. He liked her exuberance with Crissie, her nurturing spirit, her compassion, the feisty way she faced life.

He wondered if she'd bring those same attributes to bed.

Jake's wandering mind snapped to attention as Gwen suddenly froze midstep.

She called sharply to her niece, "Crissie, stop, now. Don't move. Pretend you're a statue. Whatever you do, don't move. This isn't a game. There's a snake on the path."

Jake looked in the direction of Gwen's horrified gaze. A large rattler lay on the path between the two. The day seemed unnaturally quiet. Except for the faint buzz which could be heard clear across the yard. Jake moved quickly from the corral.

"Gwen," Crissie wailed. "I don't like snakes." She took a step toward her aunt. Moving her closer to the snake.

"Mack," Jake called. "Hold Crissie." He had no idea if the dog understood him, but Mack grabbed the back of Crissie's shirt with his teeth. "Okay, pardner, stand very still. You're okay," he said in a calm voice. "Mack's with you."

He only had a second. Crissie couldn't hold still for long. He glanced at Gwen and thought his heart might stop. She was slowly walking toward Crissie. And the snake. "Gwen, stop." She took another step, her face white. And then he knew what she intended. He said the only thing which would stop her. "Hold still, Gwen. You're going to frighten the snake into striking Crissie." She froze. Jake started to tell her to back slowly away when he noticed a slight movement in the grass at the edge of the path behind her. "Don't move at all," he said deliberately, "no matter what, don't move."

Two loud shots exploded in the quiet morning, the sounds so close together the second could have been an echo of the first. Holstering the gun, Jake raced to the path. A quick check showed both snakes were dead.

Gwen stood rigid, her face bloodless. He had to deal with Crissie first. Kneeling beside her, he gave the little girl a quick squeeze before scratching Mack behind his ears. "Good dog, Mack."

"I love Mack," Crissie said. She twirled the dog's ear around her finger. Mack gave her a besotted look.

Now the danger was past, Jake's stomach turned to liquid, but he had to laugh at the dog's expression. "You and Mack are a quite a pair," he said.

Crissie smiled, having no idea why Jake laughed, but confident she and the dog had somehow pleased him. "I love you," she said. "So does Mack." She threw her arms around Jake's neck. "I didn't like the big noise."

He drew her small body against him. "I know, pardner. I didn't like to make the noise, but I had to. Those snakes could have hurt you or Gwen." He liked having Crissie seek comfort in his arms. And felt a terrible loss that he'd never hold and comfort his own child. Closing his eyes for a second, he selfishly gave himself up to the pleasure of having small arms locked around his neck.

"Snakes? More than one?" Gwen asked in a shaky voice.

Jake stood, carrying Crissie up with him. Gwen's eyes were enormous. He wanted to sweep her up in his arms with Crissie. "It's not unusual for snakes to travel in pairs." The way Gwen swallowed expressed her feelings more than words ever could.

"I wanna see snakes," Crissie demanded, recovering quickly from her fright.

Gwen shuddered. "I don't. Let's go inside and sit down."

"Let pardner see the snakes," Jake said. "She needs to know what to avoid." Bending down with the little girl, he pointed out the rattles and the patterned scales of the dead reptiles. "Never pick one of these up, pardner. Don't pick up any snake unless Gwen or an adult you trust tells you the snake is okay. You understand?''

Mack walked stiff-legged up to the dead rattlesnake. Bending his front legs, he barked excitedly at the snake. ''Mack doesn't like snakes,'' Crissie said. ''Snakes are bad.''

Jake took hold of the dog before he could grab the snake. Dead snakes still had venom. ''Snakes aren't bad. They have their purpose, but they can bite. They are scared of people and would rather run away and hide from you, but if you frighten them, they will bite you and it will hurt a lot. These fellows might have thought you and Gwen were dangerous to them, and they might have bitten you, so I had to kill them. Usually if you stand very still and then back away very, very slowly, they will crawl away. The most important thing to remember is you don't ever, ever pick one up. Okay, pardner?''

''Okay.''

Sensing Mack still wanted to make sure the snakes were dead, Jake guided the dog past the snakes and told Crissie to hold on to his collar. ''Take him to the kitchen and tell Doris what a good dog he was and what a brave girl you were. Tell her to give you some of those cookies I smell baking. And Mack gets a treat.'' He wanted them both out of the way before he gave Gwen a piece of his mind.

''Okay.''

''You'll watch where you walk, won't you, pardner?''

Crissie nodded her head violently. ''I watch for snakes.'' She tiptoed to the back door, her eyes glued to the ground.

Jake shook his head. ''I hate to scare her, but if she's going to live out here, she needs to learn to be careful. I'll clean those up, but first—'' He crossed his arms in front of his chest and gave Gwen a stony glare. ''What

the hell did you think you were doing? Never mind,''
he snarled, ''I know what you were doing. You thought
the snake would strike at something moving before he'd
strike at something standing still, so you were giving him
a moving target. What kind of crazy, damned idiot are
you?''

''I'm not an idiot. It stands to reason if he bit one of
us, it would be better to bite me. I'm bigger. It wouldn't
take much venom to...with Crissie...'' Her voice caught
and she clamped down on her lower lip.

She'd scared the hell out of him. His heart had yet to
return to normal and his stomach would never be the
same. He wanted to kick her across the barnyard for
putting herself in danger. He wanted to kiss her for being
so brave. Then he wanted to take her in his arms and
kiss her again until she promised never to do anything
like that again. He settled for yelling at her. ''That was
the dumbest, most lamebrain thing I've ever seen.
You're not even wearing boots. Do you have any idea
what rattlesnake venom can do if injected right into a
vein?''

''That would have solved your problem, wouldn't it?''

Damned woman didn't even have sense enough to admit he was right and beg his forgiveness. ''What the hell
kind of gibberish are you talking?''

''You. And Bert's gun. You shot those snakes,'' she
said accusingly.

''Yes, I shot the damned snakes.'' If he lived a hundred lives, he'd never understand this woman. ''Good
thing I wasn't expecting you to fall on my neck in gratitude,'' he drawled in a mocking voice. It dawned on
him that was exactly what he'd expected. If not for her
to fall on his neck, for her to at least see him as her hero
for saving her from a painful bite. After she begged his
forgiveness for stopping his damned heart.

"Gratitude? You expect gratitude for that?" she asked, her voice rising. "When you just did the stupidest thing I've ever seen? What were you trying to do? Kill us so you could have the ranch?"

CHAPTER NINE

"KILL you?" If she was joking, Jake wasn't amused.

"You could have shot us! Those snakes were only a few feet from us. What if you'd missed? Did you really think everyone would believe it was an accident?"

"I don't miss," he said coldly, tamping down his fury.

"I don't care how good you think you are. Everyone misses."

"I don't."

Gwen gave him the same look she'd given the dead rattlesnakes. "That's Bert's gun."

"Yes."

"You're wearing it."

"So?"

"This isn't the Old West. Why do you need a gun?"

"I was headed out to check the cattle," he explained with exaggerated patience. "If a cow's in trouble and can't be helped, it's better to put her out of her misery than make her die a painful, lingering death. Why do you think Bert had the gun?"

She gave him a long look from under her lashes. "Why don't you miss?"

"I've practiced."

"Why? So you'd be as good as your gangster relative?"

He gave her a patronizing smile. "So I'd be ready to rescue a beautiful woman in distress." Her eyes narrowed. She didn't like that answer. Even the compliment didn't appease her. She didn't like being rescued. Too bad. He'd already done it. The sure knowledge hit him

135

in the stomach with the impact of an iron fist. Hell, he
had done it. He'd rescued her. It was over then. He was
done. He'd be leaving. The pain surprised him. It wasn't
as if he'd miss her. He wouldn't. He wouldn't even remember her.

He hadn't slept with her. He never would. That's all.
He had no other regrets about leaving her.

"What's wrong?" Gwen asked.

"Nothing. Why?"

"You had an odd look on your face."

She'd probably slap his face if he told her his
thoughts. He raised an eyebrow the narrowest bit. "How
do you expect a man to look when you accuse him of
trying to murder you?" Before she could answer the
question, he pivoted on his heel and headed for the corral. "I'll be leaving soon."

"Why?"

The unexpected question caught him at the corral. He
turned. She'd followed him. "You've been firing me
since the day I arrived."

"You never paid any attention before. Why now?"
She stepped closer. "Because I accused you of trying to
kill me?"

He had to laugh. "Honey, a hundred years ago, if you
were a man, your mouth would have gotten you killed
ten times a day." His laughter died away. "As a woman,
your mouth would have gotten you ten proposals a day."
He slouched against the corral and stuck his hands in his
back pockets to keep from touching her. He took a deep
breath, inhaling her scent. Like flowers with a little spice
added.

She imitated him, jamming her hands into her back
pockets. "Do you think if I'd lived a hundred years ago,
I could have kept Jakob off the hooting trail?" She drew
in the dirt with the toe of her sandal.

Her thoughts skipped around quicker than water on a

hot skillet. "Owl-hoot trail. You'd have made it tough on Jakob to do what he had to do," he conceded. Damned tough, in fact. He eyed her curiously. "Would you have made him chose between you and doing what he felt was the honorable thing?"

"Honorable."

She couldn't have put more scorn into her answer if she'd spit in the dirt. He had an urge to laugh. An urge quickly replaced with an even bigger urge to kiss her scornful mouth. "You don't believe in honor?"

"What's honorable about running away?"

"He wasn't running away."

"Like you'd know."

"I'd know."

"How would you know?" Without warning Gwen stepped up to him and grabbed the front of his shirt, clutching it in her hands. "You don't know anything about him, remember? You'd never heard of him until I showed you the newspaper article." Tightening her fists around his shirt, she tried to shake him. "Or don't you remember that, either? You dirty, lousy, con man."

He caught her hands to save his shirt. "Let go of me."

"What if I don't? Are you going to shoot me?"

She'd tempt a saint. He was no saint. Wrapping his hands around her head, he pulled her to him and roughly covered her mouth with his, swallowing her protest. She went perfectly still, not fighting him, not responding to his kiss. For about five seconds. Then with a small sound, she threw her arms around him and practically climbed into his body, her mouth working furiously to return his kiss. Shock, then exultation, exploded in him. The same fierce sense of possession had surged through him the first time he'd sat on a hill overlooking his range, his cattle. He'd felt very king-of-the-hill then. And now. His shimmering desire for her boiled over. And merged with the satisfactory knowledge that she was his. He covered her bottom with his hands, kneading the womanly curves, feeling the heat through her jeans. When she squirmed even closer, he deepened their kiss. He'd never get enough of her.

Gwen tore away her mouth and buried her face in his chest. "I have to breathe," she muttered against his shirt.

Jake massaged her bottom with light, sure strokes. The prize was his. He could wait. Give her some time. She'd come to him when she was ready. He went very still. Time was what he didn't have. Damn Michaels. He couldn't take Jake away now.

If only Jake knew how it worked. Would he ride off on Granada and only the horse would return? Did he go to bed and the next morning the bed was empty? If Gwen stayed glued to Jake's side, would that prevent Michaels from taking him? He should have asked. He had a feeling the answer had never mattered before. Not that it mattered now. Except in the most basic of ways.

He'd never been one to hide the truth behind a glossy lie. The truth was he wanted Gwen. Period. There was nothing else. *Nada.* Women liked to pretty things up with sentimental language. They spouted drivel about love instead of admitting they wanted sex. They went on and on about love and caring and trust. Words. All words. Words they used to get what they wanted. And when they didn't want you anymore, those words were revealed for the nothing they meant.

Betrayal was the only word women should use. Betrayal is what they did best. Ma and Marian had tricked him into believing they loved him. He knew better now. And wasn't so easily tricked. He'd be long gone before Gwen got around to betraying him. But first, he'd enjoy the pleasures of her bed. Ruthlessly stamping out any vestiges of guilt, Jake told himself she'd find pleasure, too. He'd make sure of that.

A tiny shudder went through Gwen's body. She quit melting against him and took two backward steps. He rested his elbows on the top of the corral and waited for her excuse. Women always excused their passion.

"I'm sure you already know this, but I'll admit it anyway. I'm physically attracted to you. I like the way you kiss, and yes, I've come close to tearing off your clothes a couple of times, but I'm not going to." She stared fixedly at the center of his chest. "Do you want to know why?"

"Hell, yes." Should he rip her clothes off or take them off real slow, one piece at a time until she squirmed beneath him, begging him to make her his?

Her resolute gaze locked on his face. "Because it would be selfish and indulgent."

"Go ahead and use me, honey." He gave her a slow smile. "I don't mind."

She swallowed hard and looked away. "Of course you don't. I'm not stupid. I know what you want."

"Do you?" He hadn't exactly kept it a secret.

"The ranch," she said flatly. "But you can't have it. You can't seduce me into forgetting you're here to steal it. This is my home now. Mine and Crissie's. I'm going to stay here. Put down roots. I don't care how Bert's family got this ranch. It's mine now and it's going to stay mine. I'm not inviting you into my bedroom and giving you an opportunity to search for some stupid paper which you hope will prove you own this ranch."

She was like a dog with a bone, refusing to let go of her damned stupid idea. "I'm not here to steal your ranch," he said through clenched teeth. His denial merited a burning glare. His body tightened. Damn, he wanted to kiss her again.

"I may not know much about ranching, but I'm not a total imbecile. You show up out of nowhere. You pretend you know nothing about Jakob Stoner when it's obvious you know everything about him. You claim you came to work for me because you needed a job. And it just so happens you're the one person who could contest my ownership of the ranch. That's a little too much co-incidence for me to swallow.''

''The one person? What about Gordon?'' How he longed to turn her soft and clinging again.

''Gordon doesn't have a prayer of overturning Bert's will. He's nothing more than a big nuisance.''

Jake quit thinking about undressing Gwen and focused on her words. And immediately understood Michaels's plan with complete and total comprehension. He knew why Gwen needed him, and it had nothing to do with rattlesnakes. He was here to give Gwen her wish. A ranch. Her white picket fence. Roots for Crissie. She'd said it. Only one person could give her uncontested ownership of the ranch. One person. Jakob Stoner. The only question was, how was he supposed to do it?

''Marry her.''

The command came with such astonishing clarity, Jake looked around to see who'd spoken. They were alone except for Granada, who, sensing the tension in the air, stood in the corral eyeing them with a mixture of curiosity and alarm. A peach-colored butterfly lit on the water trough, then flitted over to a nodding sun-flower.

''Well,'' Gwen demanded, drawing his attention back to her, ''are you going to admit the truth or not?''

Jake gave her a lazy smile, and banked the fires of his desire. When the time came, those green eyes glaring at him would rekindle the flames quickly enough. Flames. Hell, she'd ignite a damned prairie fire. He'd have to remember to thank Michaels when he saw him. Throwing a little bonus in for Jake on his last trip. He let his gaze move leisurely, possessively over Gwen. Those curves, those eyes, that mouth promised more than a little bonus. He itched to indulge himself with a little taste of heaven, but he'd wait. She'd be worth waiting for.

"I asked you a question. I'm waiting for an answer."

He loved the way her cheeks flushed pink. She'd guessed what he was thinking. Guessed and didn't mind, no matter how much she pretended otherwise. Her body practically twanged like a taut rope. He'd mastered roping years ago. Gwen wouldn't be getting much sleep on her wedding night. Uncoiling his spine, Jake braced his shoulders and took off his hat. He'd do this right. "Miss Ashton," he said evenly, "may I have the honor of your hand in marriage?"

"You're what?"

Gwen hoped Prudence's eyes didn't pop out of her head. "Jake and I are getting married this morning." She executed a small pirouette. "How do you like my dress? It was Sara Winthrop's dress when she married Bert. Doris and I found it in the attic."

"May I see you alone for a moment, Gwen? You'll excuse us, won't you, Mr. Stoner?"

"Why sure, Ma'am," Jake drawled.

"No." Gwen put her hand on Jake's arm as he started to leave. "There's no point wasting anyone's time. You can't talk me out of it, Prudence. My mind is made up. Jake and I are getting married. As soon as we leave here, we're going over to pick up a marriage license and find a judge." She and Jake took chairs across from Prudence's desk.

"If you don't want me to talk you out of this insanity," Prudence said in a chilly voice, "I don't know why you're here." Her eyes narrowed. "If you came to ask me to be a witness, forget it. I don't push my clients in front of speeding trains."

An apt comparison, Gwen thought wryly. Only she

wasn't in front of the train, she was on it. What's more, she didn't know if she wanted off. "Tom and Doris are standing up with us. They're out in the waiting room with Crissie." Gwen hesitated. "I'd like you to come, but if you don't feel you can, I understand."

"Well, I don't understand," Prudence said. "What's the rush? What about your parents? What about Crissie's other grandparents?"

"I phoned them all last night," Gwen said. "You know my folks live in Europe. They sent me their best." Albeit reluctantly. Prudence couldn't say anything her parents hadn't already said. "As for Monica's folks, Ruth and Monk couldn't change their plans." Gwen smiled wryly at the memory of the conversation. "They're going to chant around some stone circle or something today. Ruth asked our birthdays and said somebody's in something and somebody's moon is in retrograde or whatever, and Monk dealt the tarot cards. All signs are auspicious and the karma is good or some such. They heartily approve."

"What a bunch of rot. They figure if you're married, there's no chance of you dumping Crissie on them."

"There was never any chance of that," Gwen said firmly. "Crissie is my child now, and she'll always come first with me."

Crissie was why she'd agreed to Jake's astounding proposal. She'd rejected him at first. Hadn't even believed he was serious. It had taken him two days to convince her of the practicality of his idea. She'd always been the practical one in her family.

There were sound and prudent reasons for marrying Jake. To keep the ranch. To preserve her dream. To carry out Bert's wishes. And most of all, to keep the kind of life she wanted for Crissie. That's what she told herself in daylight.

At night, in bed, she asked herself if she would have

agreed to Jake's proposal if he'd been five feet tall, bald, toothless and seventy years old. And ignored the answer. And tried to ignore the excitement licking at her veins when she thought of marriage to Jake.

Theirs would be a practical marriage. She was marrying Jake to secure her title to the ranch. Sleeping with him had never come up. She frowned. Why hadn't it come up?

"I don't blame you for worrying, Miss Owen," Jake was saying, "but Gwen is doing the right thing."

"She's marrying you, so that's obviously not true," Prudence snapped. Swiveling in her office chair, she faced Gwen. "Think about this, Gwen. He shows up out of nowhere, he might have a claim on your ranch, and you're going to marry him? Aren't you just a little worried about being murdered in your bed? It'd be an easier way to get the ranch than fighting you in court."

"That's why we're here," Jake said calmly. "We need you to draw up some papers for me to sign before we get married."

"What kind of papers?"

"I want to make out a will leaving everything I own to Gwen."

"Let me guess. Gwen does the same for you?"

"No."

If Jake objected to Prudence's offensive questions, he hid it well. He had incredible self-control. Gwen replayed in her mind the kiss by the corral. Maybe sometimes that control slipped a little. She wondered what kind of self-control he exercised in bed.

"I don't get it," Prudence said slowly.

"I don't care who Gwen leaves her belongings to," Jake said, "as long as it says in the will I have no claim to anything she owns now or at any time during our marriage."

"It's simple," Gwen added. "Jake isn't marrying me

for the ranch. I'm marrying him for the ranch. He's relinquishing any and all claim on land which may or may not have belonged at any time to his family.''

''We want another agreement, too,'' Jake said. ''One that says I'm bringing nothing to this marriage, and if we dissolve the bonds of matrimony, I take away nothing. Word it in whatever lawyer talk you want, just make sure it's watertight. I don't want anyone bothering Gwen later.''

''Later?'' Prudence asked.

''If anything should happen to me,'' Jake said.

''It'll take a while, but I should have everything ready for you to sign after your wedding. Make sure you return and sign the papers, Gwen, before you head back to the ranch. I assume there's to be no honeymoon.''

Gwen felt the heat stain her cheeks. ''Maybe later,'' she said vaguely. Why, oh why, hadn't she discussed this part with Jake? Not that she was against it. But it would be nice to know his feelings about it. She thought about his kisses and blushed redder. Cautiously she glanced at Jake, hoping he hadn't noticed. He was watching her. Something flashed across the back of his eyes. Gwen forgot to breathe. Simmering, raw, basic desire. Her entire body heated up, then Jake gave her a rueful smile. What did that mean? Whatever she thought she'd seen had disappeared. She barely heard his answer to Prudence.

''We'll go over to the café and get a cup of coffee. If we come back in an hour, will the papers be ready?'' At Prudence's nod, he said, ''The wedding can wait until then. We'll sign here before we sign at the courthouse. We'll be back in one hour.''

One hour. In one hour she intended to marry this man who'd come to steal her ranch from her. In one hour. Panic burst inside her. Jake held out his hand. Without thinking, she put her hand in his. Warmth and courage poured through her body.

"For Crissie," Jake said quietly.

"For Crissie," Gwen agreed and stood. Suddenly, inexplicably, she wanted to laugh, to sing, to dance. The wedding was for Crissie.

The wedding night was for Gwen. The wedding night. Her steps slowed. She was stark, raving mad. She couldn't marry a complete stranger. Not even to give Crissie a home.

Jake opened the office door. Crissie ran over and jumped into his arms. Gwen smiled at them, then dispensed wobbly smiles at everyone sitting in the law office's reception room. Surely all brides smiled on their wedding day.

"Second thoughts?" Jake looked at her over the top of his wineglass.

"No." Tom, Doris, and Crissie had eaten earlier, and Crissie slept soundly upstairs. "Yes. I don't know." Gwen picked at the angel food cake which had followed the fancy chicken dinner. "I told Doris not to go to any trouble, but she insisted we have some kind of private bridal dinner. I hope you don't mind."

"I don't mind."

"I tried to explain our marriage isn't quite what she thinks."

"What does she think?"

Gwen thought of Doris's teasing comments about sleeping with a stud like Jake and veered off in another direction. "Thank you for the flowers." Jake had surprised her with a huge bouquet of sunflowers he'd picked before they'd gone to town.

"Every bride should have flowers. Store-bought would have been better, but I wasn't sure I'd have a chance to buy any."

"I like sunflowers."

"I know you do." He half smiled. "I've seen you talking to them."

"They went beautifully with my dress." Gwen smoothed down the forties' style dress with its heart-shaped neckline. "I guess long, white wedding dresses with sweeping trains weren't as common in those days." Blue and lavender flowers dotted the ivory-colored satiny rayon fabric. "I wouldn't have known this was Sara Winthrop's wedding dress if I hadn't seen the note pinned to it." She couldn't stop babbling. "Sara was probably being practical. It's street-length so she could have worn it to church and stuff. That's probably why it has sleeves. For church." She grabbed her wine and drank, forcibly shutting off the mindless flow of words.

Jake leaned back in his chair. "I'm glad you left it on. I've never seen you in a dress." His mouth twitched. "I figured the sunflowers would look okay with blue jeans."

Gwen choked on her wine. "Did you really think I'd wear jeans?"

"Honey, I didn't even know if you'd show up," he drawled.

She drew a pattern with her fingernail on the white damask tablecloth Doris had unearthed. "I said I would."

"Women say a lot of things."

"That sounds very cynical. And chauvinistic." She slid a glance off him. "Have you had so much experience with women?"

"Enough."

The crisp answer told her everything. And nothing. A woman, maybe more than one, had hurt him. Marrying him to save the ranch didn't give her the right to probe old wounds. "Did she hurt you badly?"

"Who?"

"The woman who made you so cynical."

He squinted up at the chandelier hanging over the table. "No," he said slowly, "she didn't hurt me. She lied and she cheated on me by sleeping with my brother." At Gwen's tiny gasp, he looked directly at her. "But she didn't hurt me."

"Were you in love with her?"

"I'd planned to marry her."

"Did your brother know that?" At his nod, she said, "I can't imagine my brother hurting me like that."

"I told you. It didn't hurt." Jake shrugged. "She drew men to her like bears to honey. My brother was a charming, reckless, lighthearted kid. Handsome with an engaging grin and an easy way of talking to women. He collected pretty women the way Crissie picks up pretty rocks. I never should have introduced them."

"Of course you'd introduce your fiancée to your brother." She hesitated. "You said she slept with him. How did you find out?"

"She told me."

Gwen was torn between astonishment and outrage. "You've got to be kidding. That's really rotten. Was she trying to make you jealous?"

"Is that what you would do?"

"I don't play those kinds of games."

"Oddly enough, I don't think she did, either. She came to me for sympathy when he abandoned her. She told me then they'd slept together because she wanted me to make him come back to her."

"You didn't, did you?"

"I tried. He laughed at me."

"You must have hated him." At his blank look, she elaborated. "You blame her, but it takes two. Your brother stole your fiancée from you. He betrayed your trust."

"I didn't hate him."

"You said your brother died," Gwen said slowly. "Did you consider getting back together with her?"

"No."

The clipped answer spoke volumes. Jake still cared for the woman. "Maybe you should have," Gwen said hesitantly. "Maybe the thing with your brother was nothing more than a momentary aberration. Maybe you could make a go of it this time."

"She's dead," Jake said flatly.

Gwen fought an illogical urge to hold Jake to her breast and comfort him. Illogical and ridiculous. She'd never met a man as self-assured and less likely to need comforting as Jake Stoner. "I'm sorry. How terrible for you."

"Don't make it into a tragic love story," he said coolly. "I didn't love her and she didn't love me."

"You must have loved each other."

"Why must we have?"

"Well, because. You were going to be married."

Jake took a sip of his wine, his gaze never leaving Gwen's face. "You and I are married."

And what did that mean? Gwen wasn't ready to ask the question out loud. She pushed back her chair. "Doris is probably waiting for us to leave the dining room so she can clear up the dishes. I think I'll run up and see if Crissie is sleeping okay." She fled without waiting for Jake's response.

Upstairs she peeked in Crissie's room, knowing full well the little girl was sound asleep, or she would have been downstairs. Then Gwen went into the bathroom and washed her face and brushed her teeth.

Back in the hall, she stood irresolute. Jake had said nothing to indicate where he intended to spend the night. Why hadn't she stipulated something be put in the prenuptial agreement pertaining to marital relations? "The groom must attend the bride on their wedding night and so many nights a week thereafter."

Because she and Jake didn't have that kind of marriage. A marriage of convenience they used to call them. The bride had something the groom wanted and vice versa. Gwen went into her bedroom and quietly closed the door, leaning back against the paneled wood.

There were three large bedrooms and an enormous bathroom upstairs in the main house. Gwen slept in Sara Winthrop's bedroom. Bert had sheepishly admitted his snoring had meant separate bedrooms from early on in his marriage. Along with that he'd made it clear separate bedrooms hadn't meant estrangement. Gwen had a feeling the couple had practically worn a path between their bedrooms. Doris slept downstairs in her own apartment in the house's log addition. Crissie slept in what Bert had called the spare bedroom.

That left Bert's room empty for Jake.

If he wanted it.

Standing at the door, Gwen attempted to see her room through Jake's eyes. Sara's pale green wallpaper with huge white cabbage roses still covered the walls. Gwen had added the white gauzy curtains over the old wooden window blinds. The peach and cream Dhurrie rugs from India, she'd bought at a bazaar in Germany when her family had been stationed there. Childhood photos taken around the world of her mom and dad and Dan were scattered over one wall. She'd bought the southwestern picture because the mesa it depicted looked so much like the one she could see from her bedroom window. The framed print hung above the elaborate old brass bed which was covered with a green and peach quilt sewn by one of Gwen's ancestors at the turn of the century.

The last wall Gwen called her family-tree wall. Her parents and grandparents and great-grandparents, at various ages, stared from old-fashioned frames. Alongside them hung enlargements of pictures she'd found in Bert's family album. She'd been disappointed no one had labeled the photographs, but she'd attempted to identify them by their clothing. Sara she knew. Not only had Gwen seen Sara's picture all over the house when she'd visited Bert, but he'd spoken so frequently about his wife, Gwen felt she knew Sara and would have liked her very much. Sometimes she talked to Sara, told her her worries, and her dreams. Gwen looked along down the wall. The woman she thought was Bert's mother had a kind face.

Gwen's gaze went to the third woman, the woman she felt sure was Bert's grandmother. Maybe it was the limitations of early photography, but there was something unlikable about the subject. The woman, in her early twenties, was definitely a beauty with dark-colored curls cascading to her shoulders. Gwen thought the woman's eyes looked hard and greedy and her mouth petulant and discontented. It felt disloyal to Bert, or Gwen would have taken the picture down.

The woman's gaze seemed to mock Gwen. This woman would make sure her husband attended her in her bedchamber. She'd be coy, demure and ladylike, but she'd get exactly what she wanted.

Gwen's breath caught. What she wanted. The truth had stared her in the face from the moment Jake popped the astonishing question. She wanted Jake Stoner in her bed. She wanted him touching her, caressing her, kissing her.

Loving her.

Love. Such a silly word. Such a powerful word. She

loved the view out her bedroom windows. She loved sunflowers. She loved the dress she wore. She loved Crissie.

She loved Jake Stoner.

There. She admitted it. He was tall, he was good-looking, he excited her, but it was more than that. Little things. The way he smiled. One way at her, another at Crissie. His patience. With Crissie, with the horses. The way he made Gwen feel safe and secure.

Okay, he was bossy. And arrogant. Thought he knew better than her. She thought about that. Mostly he overruled her when it came to ranch stuff. Unlike some men who had to disagree with anything a woman said or suggested.

Ever since he'd moved to the ranch, she'd found herself watching for him, listening for his whistle, thinking of excuses to spend time with him. She wanted to know everything about him. There was so much she didn't know. What little information he had disclosed, she'd practically dragged out of him. He'd never be a person who blurted out his every thought or feeling.

She had no idea how he felt about her.

She had no idea if he planned to treat this marriage as a real marriage. She'd never asked the question. What if he gave the wrong answer?

What was the right answer?

She had no idea if he planned to come to her room tonight.

Gwen abandoned her post and walked slowly to her closet. He wouldn't come. She slipped out of her shoes and unfastened her bridal dress. He'd think they'd married too soon, too fast. She hung her silk slip on the hanger with the dress and removed her panty hose. He'd only married her to secure the ranch for her.

Pulling a hanger from the back of her closet, she considered what Jake expected to gain from their marriage. He'd given facile answers when she'd asked him. Answers like he wanted to repay her kindness in hiring him. She tossed her underwear on the chair. He said he wanted to settle once and for all any question of him trying to steal the ranch. He said he wanted to secure Crissie's future. The tube of cool green silk slid smoothly over her skin. Viewed with detachment, she wasn't sure his reasons added up. Addition had always been one of her major skills.

Gwen moved to the nearest window. The sun had set, but dusk lingered while a half-moon played peek-a-boo with lacy clouds. She tried to recall the saying connecting sunshine with happy brides. It hadn't rained today. From here she could see Doris's darkened quarters. The lights turning on would signal Doris had gone to her rooms for the night.

Waiting gave Gwen too much time to think. What if Jake retired for the night over at the stone house? The green nightgown displayed too much skin. Did she have the nerve to phone him, summoning him to her bed? Her breasts were too small. Men liked large-breasted women. What excuse could she possibly give to bring him back to the main house? Black would have been a better color. She didn't own a black nightgown. Black looked hideous on her.

Her jumbled thoughts drove her crazy. No light showed yet at Doris's window. This was ridiculous. Lurking like a reluctant cat burglar. Inventing more things to worry about. She needed distraction.

Padding barefoot across the room to her bed, Gwen snapped on the bedside lamp. She would read one of the journals written by the women in Bert's family. Losing

herself in another woman's life would pass the time and
settle her nerves.

Then she would go downstairs.

And seduce her new husband.

CHAPTER TEN

JAKE propped a shoulder against the stone porch pillar of the big house. The sound of clinking dishes came through the screen door. He hoped Doris worked fast. Times like this a man needed a good cigarillo, but he no longer smoked. Not that a long, skinny cigar kept a man from thinking.

And it wasn't a cigarillo he craved.

Gwen hadn't come back downstairs, which didn't surprise him. He smiled wryly in the deep dusk. Not much Gwen did surprised him anymore. Jake figured she assayed pure gold. Women like her settled this country. Came into the wilderness and made homes, raised children. Gwen was one little lady who was full of sand. She had bottom.

He shifted his weight. Having bottom used to mean a person had staying power. Gwen had that all right, but another kind of bottom came to mind. A nice, rounded one which fit perfectly into his big hands. He purely loved watching her bend over to pick up Crissie or smell a flower. She had a few other interesting parts he looked forward to fitting his hands around, too.

An early star appeared in the sky. Jake scowled at the small point of light. He had the same uneasy feeling a man on the dodge had. That the law was closing in on him. Only in Jake's case, the man, or whatever he was, on his tail was Michaels. Jake wished he had some kind of bargaining power to force Michaels to let him stay here awhile.

Desire wasn't the only thing gnawing on him. His own foolishness riled him. Why had he gone and married Gwen right away? He should have bedded her first, promising her marriage. Eventually. A man could spend a lot of nights in a woman's bed before eventually came around. Nights getting to know everything there was to know about Gwen. He reminded himself she was a woman. He'd have tired of her soon enough. Then they could have wed. And Michaels could take Jake away.

Somewhere out on the prairie a coyote threw his mocking song into the sky. Another coyote answered, then another. Men had tried to wipe out coyotes in Jake's day, yet there seemed to be more coyotes than ever. Always laughing at men for thinking they knew so much. For all Jake knew, the doglike critters were laughing at him.

He slid his left hand in his trouser pocket. If they knew his thoughts, they'd be laughing plenty. Course they'd be wrong about what they were laughing at. Sure he was acting like an anxious bridegroom. Hell, there was an attractive woman upstairs doing whatever it was women did to get ready for their wedding night.

Gwen didn't need to do a thing.

At dinner her hair had gleamed in the candlelight like gold. He'd appreciated the way the shiny dress had molded her curves. Below the sleeves, her bare arms looked as silky as the shimmering cloth. He'd been hard put not to leap over the table and press his mouth on that tantalizing spot where her dress dipped down in front. Remembering the shadowy vee and the way the candlelight caressed soft mounded flesh dried his mouth. She'd seen him staring at her and started breathing faster.

Jake adjusted his trousers and wished Doris would hurry up. Once upstairs, he didn't plan to hurry. He figured he could count on Michaels giving him one night. He planned to use every minute from now until dawn. Maybe later. No one would expect a bride and groom to get up with the chickens. Doris would take care of Crissie.

He'd take care of Gwen. She'd been nervous all day. Reminded him of a skittish filly he'd once had. Jake had gentled the filly using nothing more than his hands. He'd gentle Gwen the same way.

The need for her tightened his muscles. He had one night to satisfy that need. And an eternity to remember it.

Except he didn't. He wouldn't.

He'd never remembered before. Each of his previous trips were erased from his memory as if they'd never existed. Nine trips, Michaels had said. Nine. He remembered nothing of them. Where he'd been. Who'd he'd met. What he'd done. No matter how deeply he searched his memory, they'd vanished without a trace. As if they'd never been.

Sorrow washed over him. A sorrow he couldn't explain. He should be rejoicing. He'd done his job. He'd secured Gwen's ranch for her. Peace was in his grasp. Maybe as soon as tomorrow. Michaels would come for him and together they'd cross the great divide. To peace. Never again to be betrayed. Never again to feel pain.

The moon slid behind the clouds. Never again to hear Gwen laugh. Never again to see her green eyes shooting sparks at him. Never again to watch her walk across the ranch yard. Never again to see her smile at Crissie. Never again to touch her. Never again to kiss her.

"Jake! You'll never guess what I found."

Gwen's excited voice jerked him from his sobering thoughts. He turned around and almost fell off the porch again. She stood in the open doorway, the hall light outlining her body. A thin slip of a garment did nothing to hide her curves. Desire surged through him. He wanted to throw her down on the ground and jump on top of her. "What—" he cleared his throat "—what did you find?"

"Come see." She reached out and grabbed his arm and tugged him inside. "It's up in my room."

He climbed the stairs behind her, savoring the view. He'd been wrong. She could surprise him. She wore the most indecent nightgear he'd ever seen. He loved every square inch of it, as few square inches as there were. It took him a minute to place that particular shade of green, and then he had it. The iridescent green of a humming-bird's back. The garment's top consisted of two thin straps crossing in the middle of her back. From her waist on down the nightgown hugged her body like a lover. If it didn't take all Jake's strength to keep from taking her on the staircase, he'd laugh at her transparent method of getting him upstairs.

He'd never been upstairs, but he could explore to-morrow. If he was still around.

Gwen dashed into one of the rooms off the hall. When he followed her in, she wheeled around. "Look."

He shut the door. The framed portraits on the wall directly across the room from the doorway caught his eye. "I'll be damned," he said softly.

"Forget those pictures and look at what I found."

Ignoring her discovery for the moment, Jake walked over and pointed to one of the photographs. "Why is her portrait up here?"

"She's Bert's grandmother and Gordon Winthrop's wife. Why are you staring at her? Don't tell me you think she's beautiful?"

"Don't you?"

"Her eyes are too close together and that mouth says she's spoiled and selfish."

Jake managed not to laugh. "You don't think she looks like a blossom of western womanhood?"

When Gwen didn't answer, Jake turned to her. She

was bending over, putting a book on the bottom shelf of a small table beside her bed. The green fabric stretched over her hips outlining every curve. Jake forgot to breathe. When she straightened up and faced him, his heart almost stopped. The front of the dress revealed more than the back.

"You already knew," she said flatly. "I should have guessed."

He didn't have a clue what she was talking about. "Honey, you really know how to dress."

"Thank you. Good-night."

Jake frowned and moved toward the bed. She glared at him. Somewhere along the way, he'd taken a misstep. He felt his way cautiously. "You said you had something to show me."

"There's no point, is there? You already know."

"I think you need to chew that one a little finer for me, honey. I don't know what you're talking about."

"Marian. I'm talking about Marian."

He wanted to smile at the way she spat Marian's name, but he hadn't been born yesterday. Gwen Ashton was riled. No... "Gwen Stoner," he said softly. "I like the way my tongue fits around that."

"Don't change the subject."

"I'm not. I've had one subject on my mind all evening, and it sure isn't Marian."

"Not just Marian. Marian Winthrop. She was Mrs. Luther Stoner before she became Mrs. Gordon Winthrop. As you well know."

The cause of her anger finally sunk in. "You think I knew that?"

"You certainly recognized her picture fast enough."

He could think of no ready explanation. Not one she'd believe. "You were going to show me something."

"I've changed my mind."

"If you stick that cute little nose any further in the air, you're going to fall over the bed."

"It's not little. And if I fall over the bed, it's my problem, not yours."

He couldn't help smiling. "If you fall over the bed, that would solve my biggest problem."

"What problem could you possibly have?"

"How to get you on that bed."

"Do you really think you can romance me into forgetting what you've done?"

Jake sighed inwardly and tamped down his desire. He could toss her on the bed and in less than five minutes make her forget whatever burr she had under her saddle. He could do it, but he had a feeling she wouldn't forgive him for it. Nor would he. When he made love to Gwen he wanted the decision to be as much hers as his. Patience, he told himself. "Maybe I could answer your question better if I knew exactly what it is you're accusing me of."

"Marian." She grabbed the book from the table and tossed it on the bed between them. "It's all in that journal."

Reaching over, he picked up the book and read the dates on the spine—1918 to 1923. Jake turned the slim volume over in his hands. "Marian kept a journal?" The Marian he'd known believed reading and writing spoiled a woman's looks.

"Not Marian. Her daughter-in-law, April. Bert's mother. Go on, read it. I've marked the page."

He flipped open the journal at the marker. Elegant script covered the page. The date at the top read May 12, 1921. The ink had barely faded over time, and Jake had no trouble reading the words out loud. "'We buried Father Winthrop this morning. Decorum requires I behave as one in mourning, but inwardly I rejoice he is no longer with us. I do not know how a man whom

I disliked so intensely could sire a kind and gentle man as is my dear husband, James. I have taken pains to never let James know of the crude, unwelcome advances made to me by his own father.'''

Winthrop hadn't changed a bit, Jake thought. He read on. "'Marian plays the role of the grieving widow to the hilt, but she'll not miss him, either. I believe she truly mourned her first husband, Luther, whose name Father W. never allowed spoken in this house. Marian has mentioned Luther many times since Father W. died. I found her at my dressing table this morning using some of my face paint.'" Jake chuckled at the words in parenthesis. "'Which James does not know I use.'"

"Don't stop now. It's getting interesting."

"'When I asked her why she married Father W., the question didn't annoy her as I feared. She said she wouldn't have if Luther's brother hadn't already died, but since he had—he was shot robbing a bank!—she needed someone to take care of her and run the ranch. I would rather lose the ranch and become a schoolteacher than marry a man like Father W. should anything happen to my dearest James, but I do not think Marian has my resolution.'" Jake closed the book. "I don't think so, either. Neither can I see you marrying an old goat like Gordon."

"Of course not, because you were busy ensuring I'd marry you. There's no difference between me and Marian, is there?"

Jake's mouth fell open. "Comparing you and Marian is like—" he thought for a second "—comparing meat and potatoes and dessert."

"How charming. I assume I'm the meat and potatoes."

He winced at her tone of voice. "I meant Marian was a pretty piece of fluff. You're a woman a man can ride the river with. You have grit."

"Not to mention the old family ranch."

Jake got it then. "You think I married you to get my hands on the ranch?"

"It's rather obvious, isn't it? As long as I thought my title to the ranch was in jeopardy, you could come across as making the big sacrifice. But the truth is, you and your relatives have absolutely no claim on my—" she accentuated the pronoun "—ranch. Marian would have inherited the ranch on Luther Stoner's death. Gordon Winthrop got the ranch when he married Marian, and then it went to their son and heir, James, Bert's father. Everything nice and legal and tidy. The only way you could get your sticky hands on the land was to marry me. You're worse than Gordon Pease. He makes no bones about trying to take the ranch away from me. You crawled in here worse than those rattlesnakes you warned Crissie about. How did you put it? Snakes can bite, and their bite hurts. Well, Jake the Snake, you're through here. I'll start annulment proceedings first thing in the morning." She turned her back to him, dismissing him.

She couldn't have made him madder if she'd belted him in the gut. "Do not compare me to Gordon Pease," he said coldly.

Gwen whirled around, her face stiff with anger. "You're right. I should compare you to Gordon Winthrop. Marrying a woman for her ranch."

She could make him madder. Icy rage built within him. "If I were Gordon Winthrop," he bit out, "you'd have been on your back with your legs spread apart two seconds after I walked into this room. That would take care of any annulment."

All color left Gwen's face. "Are you threatening me?"

"Honey," he drawled softly, "when I make love to you, you'll want it as much as I do."

"I'll never want it."

He stared deliberately at the front of her gown. Her breathing quickened. The hardening tips of her breasts pushed against the slick green fabric of her gown. He lifted his gaze to her flushed face. "Liar."

She grabbed a green robe from the back of a chair. "You're the liar. Pretending you didn't come here to steal my ranch."

Jake noted with approval the robe clung to her body in all the right places. "I never told you all I know, but there's a lot about you I don't know, either. I've never lied to you," he added in a flat voice. "All right. I recognized Marian's portrait. I'd seen it years ago. She was called Marian Olson then. I didn't know who she married."

"Why pretend you'd never heard of her when you read her name in the newspaper article?"

Jake hesitated. "My stepfather always said Jakob Stoner was no good." Gwen didn't need to know Frank had been talking about his stepson when he'd said it. Jake's voice took on an edge. "That doesn't matter. What matters is I'm not here to steal your ranch. I told you from the beginning I came here to help you, and when you don't need my help anymore, I'll drift."

"I don't need your help. You can leave anytime."

Drawing her body up like some stiff-necked, shavetail cavalry lieutenant new to the West in no way subtracted from her feminine charms. Throwing back her shoulders and straightening her spine filled out the front of her gown and robe in a way which intensified the sexual need gnawing at him. Jake half smiled. He'd been granted a reprieve by Michaels. His stay here had nothing to do with the ownership of the ranch. Michaels had something else in mind. "I can't leave," he said. "You're not the one deciding when it's time." Before she could explode at that, he added, "Neither am I."

"Who then?"

"Don't really know." He smiled. "Honey, you're the only woman I know who could make opening and closing your mouth like a fish look sexy." The glare in her eyes turned to speculation. Jake wondered what she'd come up with now. She'd never bore a man.

"Is this all about sleeping with me? Is that why you married me?"

"I married you so there'd be no question about you owning the ranch." He held up a restraining hand. "Before you say it, I didn't know Marian married Gordon after Luther died. Sleeping with you is another matter altogether. It has nothing to do with the ranch or marriage or anything other than I'm a man and you're a woman and we want each other."

"I don't want you." A heartbeat later, she said, "All right, maybe I do. I like chicken-fried steak with tons of gravy, but it's bad for me so I never have it."

"I'm not bad for you."

Gwen looked directly at him. "You're not planning to stay on here. You've never planned to stay. Am I right?"

"Yes."

"And you want to sleep with me," she said slowly.

"Yes. And you want to sleep with me."

Her gaze never left his face. "If I sleep with you tonight, right now, will you stay?"

Her eyes were enormous pools of green. He'd give his right arm to be able to say yes. Not because he wanted to lie, but because in that moment he wanted to stay. To spend the rest of his life with her. A stupid desire. A weak one. He'd be giving her control. Giving her the power to hurt him. He'd never give that to another woman. Wanting her so badly had rotted his brain. She waited for his answer. "No, I won't stay if you sleep with me tonight, or tomorrow night or any of a hundred nights. I don't know when, but one day soon I'll leave here.''

She paled, but didn't look away. ''Suppose I said I was growing to care for you. Would that matter?''

''No.'' When she flinched at the curt answer, he added harshly, ''I never asked you to care for me.''

''You expect me to sleep with you and not care for you?''

''Why not? Women do it all the time.''

''I see.'' She pulled her robe tighter around her slender body. ''I can't say you didn't warn me. It was the first thing you told me. You'd be moving on. You're always moving on. Moving on so you don't care about anyone or anything. You don't want to care, do you?''

''Nope. Caring leads a man to do stupid things. I've had enough of caring, worrying and being stupid.''

The gauzy curtains at the window fluttered in the light breeze coming through the screened window. Gwen's scent came with the breeze, beckoning, enticing. He stayed put. For endless moments her gaze seemed to search the hidden corners of his soul. Then, slowly, she loosened the sash of her robe and dropped it to the floor where it puddled around her bare feet. Stepping out of the pool of green, she held out her hand to him. ''Come to bed, Jake.''

''What do you want from me?''

''Nothing. Come to bed and we'll make love.'' She started around the bed toward him.

Jake backed up until the closed door stopped his retreat. ''It wouldn't be love.'' Gwen stood in front of him, her body almost touching him. He felt her warmth. Smelled her scent.

''I'm not so sure about that, but it doesn't matter now. Too many people you've loved have hurt you, but I'd never hurt you, Jake. You can trust me.'' She reached up and untied the thin black ribbon tie at his neck. ''I can't believe how well this old long black frock coat I found fits you. It could have been tailored for you."

He'd recognized the clothes at once. Luther must have moved Jake's things into the attic when he'd moved into the house. Jake caught Gwen's hand as she started on his waistcoat buttons. He didn't dare touch her anywhere else. Not wanting her as badly as he did. First he had to think. Figure out what game she was playing. "Maybe sleeping with you isn't such a good idea."

"You're the sexiest bridegroom I've ever seen. You remind me of an old-fashioned gambler or gunfighter in this embroidered vest and that flat black hat I found." She gave him a coy smile. "You're gonna sleep with me, mister. You won me at cards, remember?" Without taking her eyes from him, she stepped back one step and slid first one thin strap, then the other off her shoulders. The gown hung for a second on her swelling breasts then slipped to the floor.

His brain, his whole body felt thick. He couldn't sleep with Gwen. Jake knew it as surely as if someone had shouted it in his ear. Once he slept with her, he'd never be able to leave her. But he had to leave her. He thought of all those who'd in some way abandoned him. He could never abandon Gwen. He could never hurt her. It had nothing to do with the fact that he'd been sent to her to help her, not hurt her. It had everything to do with Gwen. She was messing with his buttons. Messing with his self-control. He had to get away. To think. She pulled his shirt from his trousers.

He fumbled behind him for the doorknob. "I'll sleep in the bunkhouse." Jerking the bedroom door open, he fled.

Outdoors, the night air did little to cool him off. Grass rustled in the breeze and a cow mooed in the distance. What was the matter with him? He'd acted like a wet-behind-the-ears kid. If he didn't know better, he'd think he cared for Gwen. He didn't. He wouldn't. The coyotes started up their infernal yapping again. Damned stupid animals. What did they have to sing about?

Gwen closed the door to her bedroom very carefully, regardless of how badly she wanted to slam it. What she really wanted to slam was Jake Stoner's head in the door. He'd taken one look at her skinny body and run. She recognized panic in a person's eyes when she saw it. Kicking aside her nightgown, she went to the closet and grabbed a sweatshirt and a pair of sweatpants. The quilt from the bed she wrapped around her shoulders, then turned off the light and moved to the window.

Jake stood in the yard below. He didn't turn his head. She could hit him from here with a rock. If she had a rock. He'd flipped the long coat back and stuck his hands in his pants' pockets. His shoulders thrown back, he seemed to be studying the distant mesa.

The coyote serenade sent shivers down Gwen's spine. Maybe they were shivareeing the newlyweds, she thought ironically. Or laughing hysterically at humans who couldn't manage something so simple as falling into bed with one another. Coyotes didn't worry about love, did they? Maybe they did. She'd read wolves mated for life. Lucky wolves. The male wolf didn't tell the female he'd never care for her. The male wolf didn't run away.

The woman who'd hurt Jake had really done a number on him. Gwen had hoped he'd admit caring in the intimacy of bed. Not that she wanted him to lie to her so she'd sleep with him. He said he'd never lied to her. Telling her he cared wouldn't be a lie. She'd seen the look in his eyes. She'd swear he cared.

Or was it only that she wanted so much for him to care?

What did she really know about him? She knew the important things. How he was with Crissie and Mack and Doris and Tom and the horses. She knew he was an honorable man. His eyes told her that. She didn't know all the secrets from his past, but she knew the important ones. How he'd been hurt and abandoned by those who should have loved him. Maybe someday he'd tell her his other secrets. If he didn't, she wouldn't be greedy. All she wanted was his love.

Below Jake turned and walked toward the bunkhouse, taking such pains to avoid looking up at her window Gwen knew he suspected she stood there. She stood watching long after he'd disappeared through the bunkhouse door. Not that she thought he'd change his mind. She didn't even know if he'd be here in the morning. He would. He wouldn't leave without saying goodbye. Chilled, she clutched at the quilt, pulling it tighter around her. He wouldn't.

All her life she'd hated wandering from place to place. When her brother Dan had married Monica, a free spirit if there ever was one, Gwen had pitied him, but he was as much a vagabond as Monica. Only Gwen yearned for roots. Now she had them. And she'd fallen in love with a man who refused to settle down. The rolling-stone lifestyle wasn't for her and Crissie. If she couldn't persuade Jake to stay with her...

She'd manage without him. His rejecting her tonight was undoubtedly for the best. If she decided to marry again, she'd find herself a solid, sensible man who didn't care if he stirred ten feet from his home.

She half turned, leaning against the side of the windowsill. Illumination from the ranch yard light reached partially into the room, lighting Marian's photograph. The other woman smirked at Gwen. "Maybe you could have kept him," Gwen said softly, "but you wouldn't have made him happy. He's a strong man who needs a strong wife. If he'd stay, I could make him happy."

He had no intention of staying.

Hours later, Gwen lay awake in bed, staring at the ceiling, still wearing the sweat suit and wrapped in the quilt. If she'd hoped Jake would change his mind and return, she no longer indulged in such foolishness. She'd long ago admitted the reason she couldn't sleep was because she was afraid if she shut her eyes, when she opened them in the morning, she'd find Jake had gone.

Mack whined outside the bedroom door. Gwen got up and opened it. "Come in to keep me company?"

He whined again.

She sighed. "I thought big dogs could go all night without having to go out." The coyote chorus had stilled long ago. Gwen padded down the staircase, the dog beside her, his nails tapping loudly in the quiet house. Taking care her quilt didn't drag on the floor, Gwen opened the front door and followed the dog outdoors. The night was mild. She'd sit on the porch bench and wait for him. Mack stood sentinel on the porch, his muzzle pointed toward the road. "C'mon, Mack, do your thing, and let's get back in the house."

Mack growled softly, then walked stiff-legged down the porch steps. Preoccupied with her thoughts, the significance of the raised ruff on Mack's back didn't immediately hit Gwen. When it did, she jumped to her feet and reached out to grab the large dog. She missed. He shot from the porch and sped across the yard and down the road. Gwen dropped the quilt, dashed into the house to jam her feet into Bert's old boots and lifted down the old buffalo gun hanging on the wall. Whoever was messing with her horses didn't need to know the gun wasn't loaded. She ran out of the house, detouring by the bunkhouse to bang on the door, then took off running as fast as she could in Mack's wake.

By the time she spotted the vehicle a quarter of a mile down the road, footsteps pounded distantly behind her. Ahead of her Mack erupted in a frenzy of barking. He'd found the intruder. A man's voice screamed obscenities. Gwen recognized the voice. Her eyes growing accustomed to the dark, she saw Mack streaking toward the man. Moonlight bounced off the metal object the man pointed at the dog.

"Mack, stop!" she screamed. "Stay!" Hearing her voice, Mack hesitated. His frantic barking continued unabated. Shouts came from behind Gwen. Dropping the buffalo gun, she lunged for the dog, succeeding in catching him around the neck. "Get out of here, Gordon. Quick. I won't be able to hold him long. Don't come back or I'll call the sheriff."

The man-shaped shadow didn't move for a long moment. Finally he turned to leave. Mack burst from Gwen's hold. Gordon whirled, his arm outstretched. He was going to shoot Mack. Gwen screamed and leaped for the dog, barely managing to latch on to his rear end. As he squirmed to get loose, someone hurtled past, shoving her and the dog hard to the ground. The sound of a gunshot cracked the night.

Gwen struggled for air, the breath having been knocked out of her by the hard fall. She couldn't speak.

Gordon swore and ran. Summoning all her energy, Gwen screamed at Gordon to come back. A car door slammed, the engine started, and the pickup disappeared in the distance.

Clouds blotted out the moon. Gwen strained to hear. Only her breathing broke the stillness of the dark, oppressive night. "Mack? Jake? Tom? Doris? Who's there?" Silence answered her. Pulling herself to her knees, Gwen groped frantically around on the ground. She bumped into Mack first. Passing her hands over his body, she found no evidence of any wound. His heart beat steadily, yet the dog lay motionless. She felt his head and scraped her hand on the rock under his ear. He

must have landed on it and been knocked unconscious.
She could do nothing for him now.

She had to find Jake. She knew he'd been the one
who'd pushed her down. The gunshot echoed ominously
in her brain. Crawling carefully, she headed hopefully
in the right direction. Her knee ran into a man's boot.
"Jake?" He didn't answer. Half numb with fear, she ran
shaking hands slowly over his body. "Jake, wake up.
Jake, talk to me."

Warm liquid on his chest oozed between her fingers.
The moon slowly emerged from hiding to show her a
spreading darkness. Terror lodged in her throat. "No,
Jake, no. Don't die. You can't die." Yanking her sweatshirt over her head, she folded it and pressed it cautiously to his chest. She had to go for help. She didn't
want to leave him. Carefully she folded his arms over
his chest to hold the sweatshirt in place. Her eyes grew
gritty with unshed tears. There wasn't time to cry.

Gwen forced herself to her feet. One of her boots had
fallen off. She couldn't stop to look for it. A hoof struck
a rock. The horses. Looking toward the pasture, Gwen
saw the dark shapes milling nervously around. Bert had
told her the smell of blood frightened horses. If she
could catch a horse, she'd reach the house much quicker.
Stumbling to the fence Gwen tried to whistle. Only air
passed her lips.

"Vegas, Susie, please, come help me. Please." One
shadow detached itself from the others and pranced ten-
tatively toward her, snorting anxiously. Gwen's heart almost failed her when she recognized Granada, the big
horse Jake rode. The horse Bert had called the greenest,
wildest horse he owned. Granada would never allow
Gwen near him. And if he did, she couldn't get on him,
much less ride him.

She slipped between the two upper strands of barbed
wire. "Okay, Granada, you have to help me." A sob

caught in her throat. No, she couldn't cry. Not now. Granada was too tall. Scratching his neck and grabbing his mane, she tugged him toward a large, nearby rock. To her surprise he came along. Scrambling up on the rock, Gwen held on to the gelding's mane and pulled herself up on his back. If she couldn't stay on...

She would stay on. She had to. For Jake.

He wasn't dead. He wasn't.

CHAPTER ELEVEN

"HAVE some hot coffee. You look like you could use it."

Gwen looked up and took the steaming paper cup from Prudence. "Thanks." It gave her something to hold on to. "How did you know I was here?"

"Doris called me." Prudence sat in the chair next to Gwen. "She said to tell you Crissie is still sleeping and Tom says Mack is a little groggy, but he's going to be fine."

"He crawled over and put his head on Jake's chest," Gwen said dully. "Helped stop the bleeding. I had to leave Jake."

Prudence touched Gwen's knee. "Doris told me. You did the right thing. You saved his life."

"Did I? Nobody will come and tell me. They've been in there hours." Her voice rose in pitch. She saw a man in the emergency waiting room look her way. She swallowed hard. Hysteria wouldn't help Jake. "It seems like hours." Stretching her feet out in front of her, Gwen absently noted she wore one of Bert's old boots and one of her tennis shoes.

"Would you like me to get you something to wear?" Prudence asked. "Maybe a comb and some makeup?"

"Why? Would that help Jake? Will he live or die depending on whether I look like a fashion plate?"

"I thought you might be more comfortable in something other than Bert's old slicker. Why are you wearing it, anyway? Are you cold?"

Gwen looked down at the yellow garment she clutched around her. "I don't have anything on under it.

172

I used my sweatshirt for..." She couldn't continue. "After I called emergency, I guess this was the first thing I grabbed. I had to get Tom and go back to Jake."

Prudence reached for the wobbling paper cup of coffee and set it on the side table. She took Gwen's hand. "Do you want to tell me what happened?"

"No, I can't." Gwen clung to Prudence. "I've already talked to the sheriff. The hospital called him. I can't tell it all over again."

"All right."

"It was Gordon. I recognized his voice. Somebody cut the fence once before, but I never thought of Gordon," Gwen said. "The sheriff came back and told me. Gordon was so scared he spilled his guts." Terror exploded in Gwen's brain. "Jake spilled everything. So much blood. Gordon shot him."

"Jake will be fine. You don't have to talk about it."

"No, I can't talk about it." Releasing Prudence's hand, Gwen pulled at the knee of her sweatpants. "Gordon brought a gun this time. To shoot Mack with. But I called him by name so he wasn't going to, but then Mack went for him and he started to shoot him and I grabbed Mack and Gordon was going to shoot anyway and he would have shot me and I should be in there being operated on but Jake shoved Mack and me out of the way and he took the bullet Gordon meant for Mack or maybe he meant it for me." Gwen stopped to breathe. "I never dreamed Gordon was dangerous."

"Me neither. I can't bear to think about it."

"We can talk about something else," Prudence said gently. "Or not talk, if you prefer."

"Not talk. I'm too worried to talk. I can't think." Gwen pulled at the fabric on her other knee. "Gordon was drunk when the sheriff found him, so who knows what he meant, but I would have been shot except Jake got in the way, he always does that, has to do things his

way, always thinks he knows best and getting shot serves
him right because he should have let me do it my way
and I could have been shot and if I hadn't let Mack out
none of this would have happened and I shouldn't have
called Jake when I went after Mack because I know Jake
always has to do things his way and he thinks he knows
everything and now he's been shot—'' Gwen came to a
full stop at the last word. The sound of the gunshot reverberated painfully in her head. Rubbing her hands together she tried in vain to remove the remembered feel
of Jake's blood seeping through her fingers. Not all the
soap in the hospital could remove that.

''Mrs. Stoner?'' A man in green stood in front of
Gwen. ''I've just come from surgery. Your husband is
in recovery.''

''He's okay? Oh, thank you, Doctor, thank you.''

The doctor frowned. ''He made it through surgery, but
the next few hours will tell the story.''

Gwen pulled the slicker tighter around her in the suddenly chilled room. ''What does that mean?''

''In all honesty, Mrs. Stoner…'' He hesitated.
''There's a lot we don't know about the human spirit. It
may depend on how badly your husband wants to live.
I've seen worse injuries where the patients recovered.
And from his scars, I'd say your husband is pretty tough.
Meanwhile, we're doing all we can for him.''

''May I see him?''

''Not yet. Someone will tell you when.'' In the doorway, he turned back to her. ''You might pray for him,
Mrs. Stoner. Doctors do what we can, then we hope for
miracles.''

Music woke Jake. Crystalline notes of such exquisite
beauty he opened his eyes in search of the musician. A
tunnel of shining white beckoned irresistibly to him.
Jake stepped hesitantly into the soft swirl of clouds. No

floor supported him, but he sensed no danger of falling. Peace and joy bathed his limbs, washing the pain from his chest. An uneasy sensation nagged him from behind, but he ignored it as the far end of the tunnel pulled him compellingly toward it.

A man stood in the mouth of the tunnel. Drawing near, Jake recognized Michaels. A different Michaels. Gone were the bowler hat and string tie. This Michaels wore a long robe of bright, luminous white. "What's going on? Where am I?"

"Your work on earth is done. Congratulations, Jakob. You've earned the right to be here." Michaels chuckled. "As you humans like to say, you've earned your wings."

Pleasure and satisfaction flowed through Jake's veins. Then, faintly, he heard his name called. Frowning, he looked around for the caller. He stood in the midst of a thick fog, so dense he should have felt cold drops of moisture, but he felt only warmth. He saw no one. He and Michaels stood alone. Once more Jake felt an uneasy, nagging sensation. As if he'd forgotten something. He heard his name again. Fainter this time, yet the call disturbed him. "Did you hear that?"

"Hear what?" Michaels asked serenely.

Jake had never seen Michaels like this. The harsh, uncompromising judge had been transformed into an angelic presence from whom flowed tranquility and comfort. Jake's cares and concerns ebbed away. He'd found peace. "Nothing," he said. "I don't hear anything now." Michael's body wavered around the edges and disappeared into the mist. Only his face remained clearly defined. He didn't appear to move, yet Jake felt a touch on his arm.

"Come," Michaels said. "Everyone is waiting."

"Yes," Jake said, "I hear her calling." He stopped

walking with Michaels. Something held him back. "I hear her again. It's Gwen. Where is she?"

"It's not her time, Jakob. You did what you were sent to do. Someone messed up and Crissie's parents died before their time. You were sent so Crissie would have someone. You saved Gwen's life."

"This time. What about next time? Gordon Pease meant to shoot her. He wants the ranch. Next time he might kill her."

"She's safe. She recognized his voice and told the authorities. They've already found him."

"He confessed?"

Michaels's eyes flashed. "Yes. His advocate advised against it, but Gordon was granted an instant of seeing into his own darkened soul and in that instant he saw what envy and avarice had lowered him to. He'd bought the gun to use against the dog, but when Gwen called him by name and the dog charged him, Gordon panicked. He tried to convince himself and the authorities he was aiming at the dog, but the shock of actually killing a man may eventually save Gordon from eternal darkness. He admitted he went crazy for a second and thought if he killed Gwen, not only would no one know he'd been there, he'd inherit his uncle's estate."

"Gordon killed a man?"

Compassion shone on Michaels' face. "He killed you, Jakob."

"Me. Then I'm really dead," Jake said flatly.

"As you wished. You no longer have to walk among men who lie and cheat and steal and maim and kill."

"They're not all like that. Gwen's not. And Crissie."

Light, airy wings flashed from nowhere to gleam in the soft light. "Two people, out of a multitude of men with evil in their hearts. You said it yourself. There's no hope for humans."

"I was wrong. A person can make a difference by doing what's right."

Michaels gave him an arch look. "You don't really believe that, do you, Jakob? You tried to save Luther and he laughed at you and continued his outlaw ways. You saved that child after the bank robbery and got yourself killed. You married Gwen because you thought doing so would save her ranch, and she accused you of trying to steal the ranch. How many times have you cursed yourself for not minding your own business?"

"Am I to be punished for being wrong?"

"Punished?" Arms unfolded from the glittering light and spread wide in an expansive gesture. "Most people don't consider coming here as punishment. Up here we have only beauty and peace and love."

The clouds disappeared. Jake stood at the edge of a spectacular field of Texas bluebonnets dotted with scarlet Indian paintbrush. In the middle of the field his pa and ma, their arms entwined, waited under a huge cypress tree. Luther stood at their mother's side. Jake heard a giggle of laughter and looked above his brother's head. A red-haired sprite bouncing on a child-size cloud waved at him. Except for the tiny white wings sprouting from her back, she reminded him of Crissie.

Luther grinned ruefully. "Howdy, Jake. Betcha never thought you'd see me here. When you died saving that kid, I saw what I'd become. Thanks, brother."

Jake's mother repeated his name over and over. Tears streamed from her eyes. His father hugged her close and gave Jake a look filled with meaning. Jake understood his father was telling him his mother had done her best, and wasn't to be blamed for her weakness. Pa wanted Jake to let go of his anger and hurt and hatred. Jake looked at his mother, then slowly gave her a loving smile. Her tears turned to tears of joy. He knew then Ma had loved him as best she could. Love radiated from his family, embracing him with warmth and happiness.

"Your family's been waiting a long time for you, Jakob. Everyone's here. Everyone you love."

The distant voice called his name again. Much fainter, yet the call tugged at him, and he knew. Not everyone he loved was here. "I have to go back."

"Go back, Jakob? Why? You've worked hard to get here. You deserve your reward. What's back on earth but stupidity, pollution, crime, wars, evil? Going back to your ranch would mean hard work, floods, droughts, blizzards, taxes, politicians, and no guarantee of success."

"I wouldn't be fighting alone. Who do I talk to about going back?"

Michaels smiled, a smile of intense sweetness. "You talk to yourself, Jakob. The choice is up to you. If you want to go back—" he spread his hands wide "—then go."

"For how long?"

"For the rest of your life. How long that will be..." Michaels shrugged. His wings shimmered in the brilliant light. "I can't tell you that. I can only tell you what we whisper to every baby. Live. And love."

Halfway to the tunnel, Jake remembered his family. He turned. They waved to him, then gradually faded until only a swirling mist marked their leaving. For a moment, Jake wavered. The sound of his name came again. Gwen. At the entrance to the tunnel, Jake stopped. Michaels stood there. "You don't seem surprised," Jake said. "Did you know I'd want to go back?"

"Yes, Jakob. I knew."

Michaels's image blurred until there was no man, no angel, only a glowing cloud of phosphorus. White, yet filled with gold and silver and the colors of the rainbow and all the colors of earth and sky and all the colors that ever were and ever will be. From the center of the light came a quiet laugh. "You see, Jakob, I met Gwen in your hospital room."

Jake turned and heard his name. Weaker this time. Gwen needed him. He walked into the tunnel, slowly at first, then faster and faster until he was running harder than he'd ever run in his life.

She sat quietly at the side of Jake's bed in intensive care. Hours had passed since he'd come out of surgery. Hospital personnel flowed in and out of the room. Gwen read in their eyes the answers to the questions she feared to ask. Prudence had carried in food fixed by Doris and delivered to town by Tom. Prudence had also brought shoes and clean clothes, but terrified he'd die in her absence, Gwen refused to leave Jake's side even for the few minutes it would take to clean up and dress.

With one hand she gripped Jake's hand as tightly as she dared. Her other hand clutched a picture Crissie had drawn and sent to Jake. The three of them on the Ferris wheel. All the faces, even Gwen's, wore enormous smiles.

When they'd first permitted her to see Jake, Gwen had cried. She had no tears left. He lay so still, so lifeless. Initially she'd watched the machines with their fluctuating lines and blinking lights, but she could no longer bear the sight of them. She wouldn't need a machine to tell her Jake had died. She'd know. Except he wasn't going to die. She wouldn't let him. He couldn't die. She'd never told him she loved him. She couldn't let him leave her. She wouldn't let him go.

"I'm your wife, Jake, your wife. I need you. Crissie needs you. We love you. Jake, come back to me. Don't leave me, Jake. Don't leave. I don't care about your past, your secrets. I love you, Jake. I need you. Jake, please, come back. Don't die. Darn you, I won't let you die.

Jake, you have to live. Jake, Crissie and I need you. I love you, Jake. You have to live, Jake, live.''

The very air in the room stilled. At that instant, she knew. Pain and despair ripped through her. She didn't have to read the machines to know. Jake had left her. She was alone. She'd call the nurses in a minute. They knew. They were outside watching the machines. She needed a minute to say goodbye. A single tear ran down her cheek. ''I loved you, Jake. I loved you and I never told you. I'm so sorry I never told you. Maybe you wouldn't have cared.''

Gwen hadn't seen him come into the room, but a doctor dressed in green operating clothes leaned over Jake. His name tag read ''Michaels.'' She hadn't seen him before. Wordlessly Gwen looked at the doctor, willing him to say the words she longed to hear. Willing him to say the words she knew it was too late to say.

He smiled at her and nodded toward the drawing she held. ''She's quite an artist.''

The doctor had the kindest eyes Gwen had ever seen. He was reminding her, even if she'd lost Jake, she still had Crissie. Gwen held out the crayon picture. ''It was a happy day.''

''I can see that.'' He took the picture in his hand.

''She loved him. He was so good with her. And with animals. And brave. He saved my life. Not because I'm his wife or because he loved me, but because that's the kind of man he is. Was. A strong man.''

''I'm sure Jakob loves you.''

''Yes, I think he does. I mean, I know he did. He didn't know it.'' She gave a hiccuping laugh. ''That sounds silly, doesn't it? But it's true. I don't know her name, but she was stupid. A woman doesn't throw away a good man like Jake.''

''You wouldn't throw him away.''

''Never. Well, I fired him lots of times, but he never

left. I never wanted him to leave.'' Gwen smiled ruefully. ''I have a temper sometimes.''

''None of us are perfect.''

''True. Jake wasn't. He was bossy and arrogant, and
always thought he knew best.'' She ought to leave. Let
the doctor do his thing. Talking to him comforted her.
She'd leave in a minute. It wouldn't matter to Jake. Not
now. Gwen cleared her throat. ''He saved my life.''

''I know. Now your dreams can come true. Your
ranch, a home, the important things.''

She didn't question how he knew. The sheriff had
been in and out. There was bound to be talk throughout
the hospital. ''I never had a home,'' she said. ''We were
always moving. I didn't want that for Crissie, but it
doesn't really matter now. Getting what you want isn't
always what it's cracked up to be.'' She closed her eyes
briefly. ''Jake would have made a wonderful father.''

''You love him very much.''

''Yes.'' Her fingers spasmodically twisted in the bed-
sheet. ''I never told him. Can you believe it? Not even
on our wedding night. Do you think he knew?''

''I'm sure he knows.'' The doctor stood back from
the bed. ''I'm not really supposed to say this, but I think
Jakob is going to be just fine.''

''What did you say?'' Gwen managed in a quavering
voice. She couldn't possibly have heard correctly. Jake
had died. She'd felt his spirit leave the room. She'd felt
the cold, the emptiness. ''He's—he's going to be all
right?''

The doctor chuckled. ''He'll probably still be bossy
and arrogant and think he knows best, but I have a feeling you can handle him.''

The exquisite relief drained all blood, all sensation
from her body. Gwen slumped in her chair, unable to
speak, to think. She could barely breathe. Jake still lived.

She needed reassurance and opened her mouth to ask again. The doctor had gone.

Gwen blinked. Maybe she'd dozed off. Maybe no one had been there. She wanted so badly for Jake to live, her imagination had conjured up a doctor to tell her the words she desperately longed to hear. Cautiously, fearfully, she turned her head and cried out when she saw the lines zigging and zagging across the screen. Strange, jagged, precious lines registering Jake's every heartbeat.

Jake's death had been a nightmare, nothing more. No doctor had come in. She'd dreamed the kindly man who hadn't looked at Jake's chart or glanced at the machines. He hadn't checked Jake's chest. She'd dreamed he'd slowly moved his hands up and down the length of Jake's body about six inches above the blankets.

A piece of paper on the other side of Jake's hospital bed caught her eye. Crissie's picture. How had it gotten there? She thought of her phantom doctor taking the picture from her and looking at it. No. A stray breeze. While she'd dozed. Her hand had relaxed and a breeze from the ventilator or something had caught the paper and lifted it across the bed.

Her gaze slowly moved to Jake's face. She'd swear he had more color. His breathing sounded less labored. She must have noticed those things in her dozed state. Hope crept in to warm the edges of her heart. Treacherous hope.

Surrendering to exhaustion, she rested her head on the bed beside Jake's tanned hand and pressed a kiss to his palm. "Damn you, Jake Stoner, don't give up. Fight. You have to want to live."

"Whatever you say, boss lady."

Gwen lifted her head. Jake gave her a smile of exquisite beauty. She was wrong. She did have tears left. "I love you," she whispered.

He caught a tear running down her cheek. "If you

really do, you'll go on a midnight ride with me wearing what you wore tonight.''

"A sweat suit?"

"Without the top." He wiped away another tear. "I came to for a minute and saw you on Granada. Next time I want to be able to do something about it."

She barely blushed. "I'll ride stark naked if you want."

Jake chuckled. "There's a promise I plan to hold you to, Mrs. Stoner."

"Jake." Gwen grabbed a paper tissue, blew her nose hard, then looked squarely at him. "If you want to move on, I won't stop you." She took a deep breath. "There's just one thing you ought to know. Crissie and I are going with you."

Jake contemplated her slicker. "You're not going anywhere," he said absently. "You got anything on under that?"

"No, yes, sweatpants. I mean it, Jake. I don't care where we go, or how often we move. I was wrong about Crissie needing a place to put down roots. She doesn't need a building. She needs a home. My mother used to tell me wherever we lived was home, but I didn't understand then. I do now. A home isn't four walls and a roof. A home is family. It's love. I love you, Jake Stoner. If you want to go to Timbuktu, or the ends of the earth, I'm going along. Home is where you are." Her ringing declaration bounced off the hospital room walls. "Darn you, Jake Stoner, don't you have anything to say?"

"Yes, Ma'am, boss lady. I'm letting you lay down the law about that, because I already decided I'm staying. A man doesn't walk away from the love of a good woman. Not when he loves her."

Fresh tears sprang to Gwen's eyes. "Jake," she said helplessly.

He gave her that slow, sexy smile which liquefied her

insides. "Now I've got a couple of questions. You think there's a lock on that door?"

"Why do you need..." She saw the gleam in his eyes. "Jake Stoner, you're hooked up to a million machines. You start even thinking about what I think you're thinking about and every nurse in the hospital will rush in here to see why those machines are going haywire."

"Well, then, honey," he drawled, "you better call one of those damned nurses and get me out of here. I want to go home. This is my wedding night."

"Your wedding night was last night, and you're not going anywhere. You were shot." She lovingly brushed his hair off his forehead. "You said you had a couple of questions. What's the other one?"

"How high do you want that damned white picket fence?"

"Don't you mean double-dog damned white picket fence?"

"Listen, honey, pardner doesn't like it when you use bad words. Didn't I warn you what was going to happen the next time you said one?"

She was right about the machines bringing the nurses on the run.

Harlequin Romance ®

Invites You to A Wedding!

Whirlwind Weddings
Combines the heady romance of a whirlwind courtship with the excitement of a wedding—strong heroes, feisty heroines and marriages made not so much in heaven as in a hurry!

Some people say you can't hurry love—well, starting in August, look out for another selection of fabulous romances that prove that sometimes you can!

THE MILLION-DOLLAR MARRIAGE by Eva Rutland—
August 1998

BRIDE BY DAY by Rebecca Winters—
September 1998

READY-MADE BRIDE by Janelle Denison—
December 1998

Who says you can't hurry love?

Available wherever Harlequin books are sold.

HARLEQUIN®
Makes any time special ™

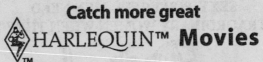 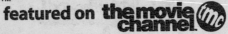

Mysterious, sexy, sizzling...

THE AUSTRALIANS

Stories of romance Australian-style, guaranteed to
fulfill that sense of adventure!

This November look for
Borrowed—One Bride
by Trisha David

Beth Lister is surprised when Kell Hallam kidnaps her on her
wedding day and takes her to his dusty ranch, Coolburna. Just
who is Kell, and what is his mysterious plan? But Beth is even
more surprised when passion begins to rise between her and
her captor!

*The Wonder from Down Under: where spirited women win
the hearts of Australia's most independent men!*

Available November 1998
where books are sold.

HARLEQUIN®
Makes any time special ™

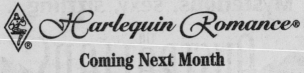

Harlequin Romance®

Coming Next Month

#3527 THE VICAR'S DAUGHTER Betty Neels
It took a tragic accident to bring plain, sensible Margo an offer of
marriage from Professor Gijs van Kessel. It was a practical proposal,
but, as Margo was taken into the bosom of his family in Holland, she
did wonder whether he might, someday, return her love....

#3528 HER MISTLETOE HUSBAND Renee Roszel
Third book in this magical trilogy
Elissa Crosby had assumed a mothering role with her two younger
sisters for years. Stubborn and independent, she couldn't confess that
her mystery Christmas guest was not the affectionate lover they
assumed, but a man who threatened to take away everything she held
dear....

Enchanted Brides—*wanted: three dream husbands for three loving
sisters.*

#3529 BE MY GIRL! Lucy Gordon
Nick Kenton had a perfectly ordered life—until Katie Deakins came to
stay. Instead of the gawky teenager he remembered, Katie was now a
stunningly beautiful woman. Worse, she was a beautiful woman intent
on turning his life upside down!

Bachelor Territory—*there are two sides to every story...and now it's
his turn!*

#3530 WEDDING BELLS Patricia Knoll
Brittnie wished her relationship with Jared Cruz extended beyond that
of boss and employee—and involved marriage! At first Jared wasn't
interested. But then his grandfather decided to play cupid, and Jared
found himself having to think again....

Marriage Ties—*four Kelleher women bound together by family
and love.*